AMELIA
RULES

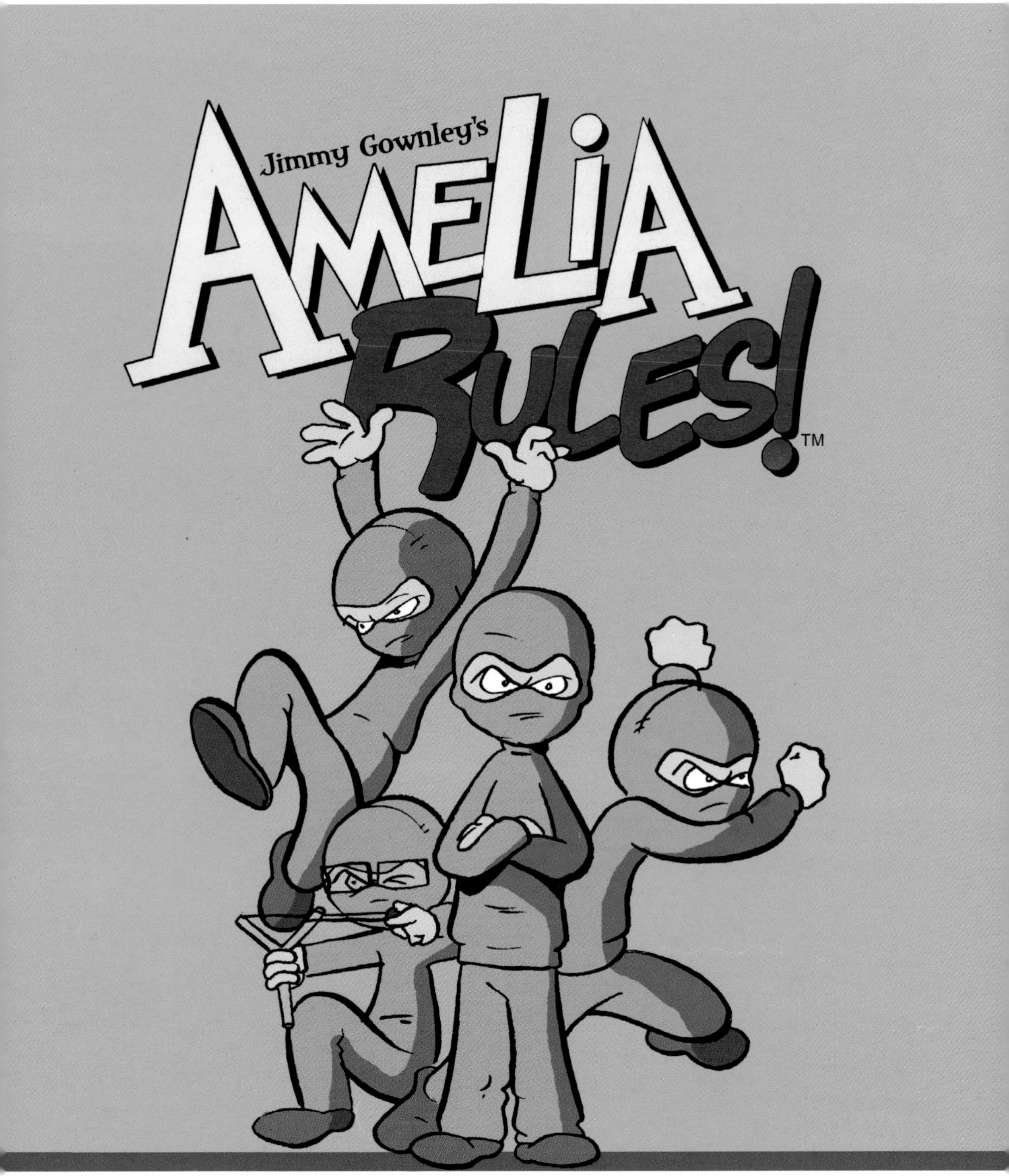
Jimmy Gownley's
AMELIA RULES!™

Joy and Wonder

Atheneum Books for Young Readers
New York London Toronto Sydney
Spotlight

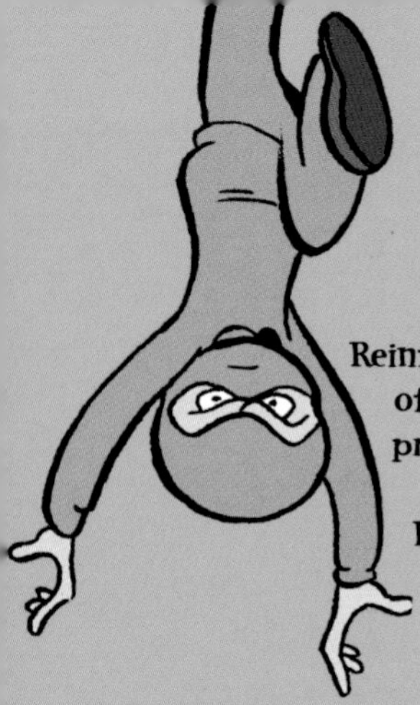

visit us at www.abdopublishing.com

Reinforced library bound edition published in 2013 by Spotlight, a division of the ABDO Group, PO Box 398166, Minneapolis, MN 55439. Spotlight produces high-quality reinforced library bound editions for schools and libraries. Published by agreement with Atheneum Books for Young Readers, an imprint of Simon & Schuster Children's Publishing Division.

Printed in the United States of America, North Mankato, Minnesota.
102012
012013
This book contains at least 10% recycled materials.

· Special thanks to Michael Cohen ·

Book design by Jimmy Gownley and Sonia Chaghatzbanian

Library of Congress Cataloging-in-Publication Data

Gownley, Jimmy.
Amelia in joy and wonder / [Jimmy Gownley]. -- Reinforced library bound ed.
p. cm. -- (Jimmy Gownley's Amelia rules!)
Summary: When Amelia and her friends tag along on Aunt Tanner's business trip to New York City, Amelia gets to visit with her father and best friend, Sunday Jones, and learns a lesson about home.
ISBN 978-1-61479-072-3
[1. Graphic novels. 2. Home--Fiction. 3. Friendship--Fiction. 4. Fathers and daughters--Fiction. 5. Aunts--Fiction. 6. New York (N.Y.)--Fiction.] I. Title.
PZ7.G69Amo 2013
741.5'973--dc23

2012026911

Spotlight

All Spotlight books are reinforced library bindings and manufactured in the United States of America.

To my beautiful girls:
Stella Mary and
Anna Elizabeth,
And to their wonderful mother, Karen.

You're what make ME happy.

MEET THE GANG

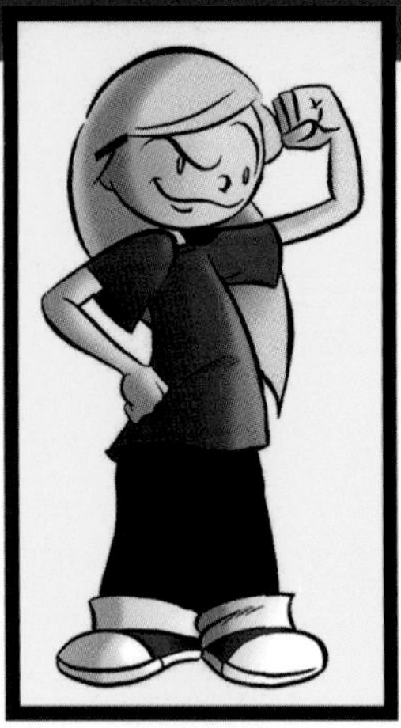

Amelia Louise McBride:
Our heroine. Wise cracking, yet sweet. She spends her time hanging out with friends and her aunt Tanner.

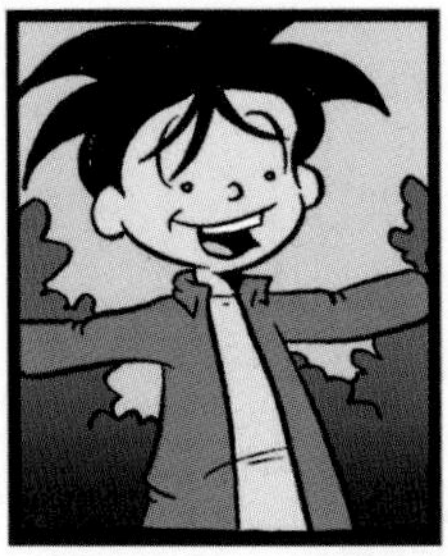

Reggie Grabinsky:
A.k.a. Captain Amazing. Founder of G.A.S.P., which he forces . . . er, encourages, his friends to join.

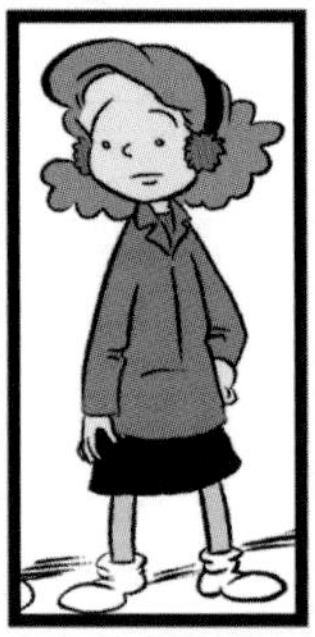

Rhonda Bleenie:
Smart, stubborn, and loud. She wears her heart on her sleeve and it's filled with love for Reggie.

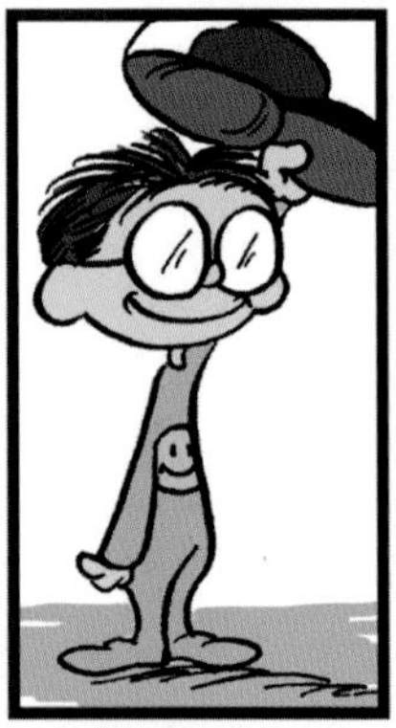

Pajamaman:
Never speaks. Always cool. His feetie jammies tell you what's on his mind.

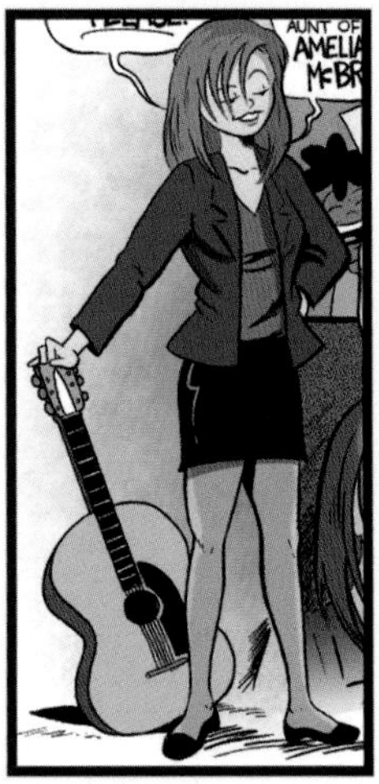

Tanner:
Amelia's aunt and a former rock 'n' roll superstar.

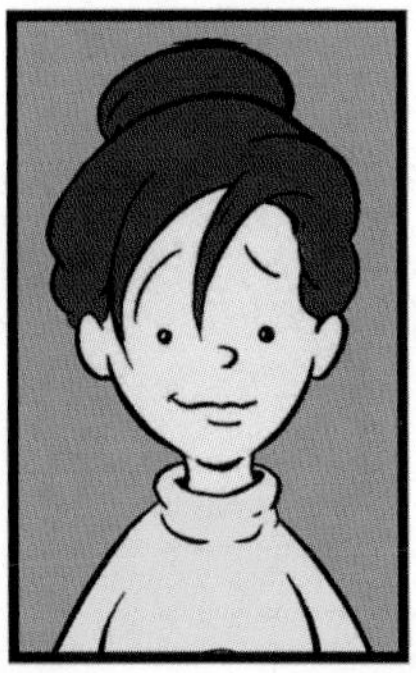

Amelia's Mom (Mary):
Starting a new life in Pennsylvania with Amelia after the divorce.

Amelia's Dad:
Still lives in New York, and misses Amelia terribly.

G.A.S.P.
Gathering Of Awesome Super Pals. The superhero club Reggie founded.

Park View Terrace Ninjas:
Club across town and nemesis to G.A.S.P.

Kyle:
The main ninja. Kind of a jerk but not without charm.

Joan:
Former Park View Terrace Ninja (nemesis of G.A.S.P.), now friends with Amelia and company.

Tweenie Zeenie:
A local kid-run magazine and Web site.

tweeniezeenie.com

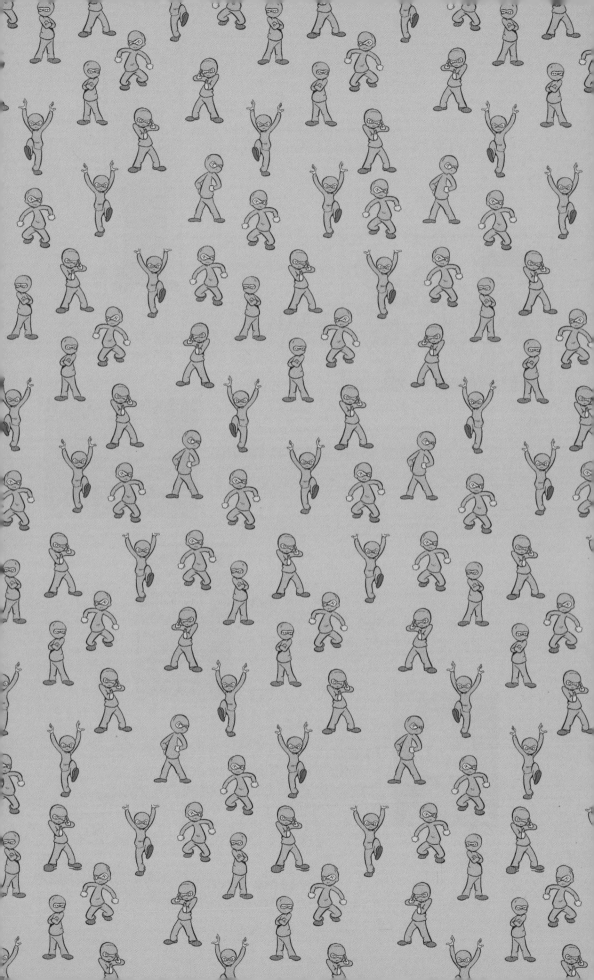

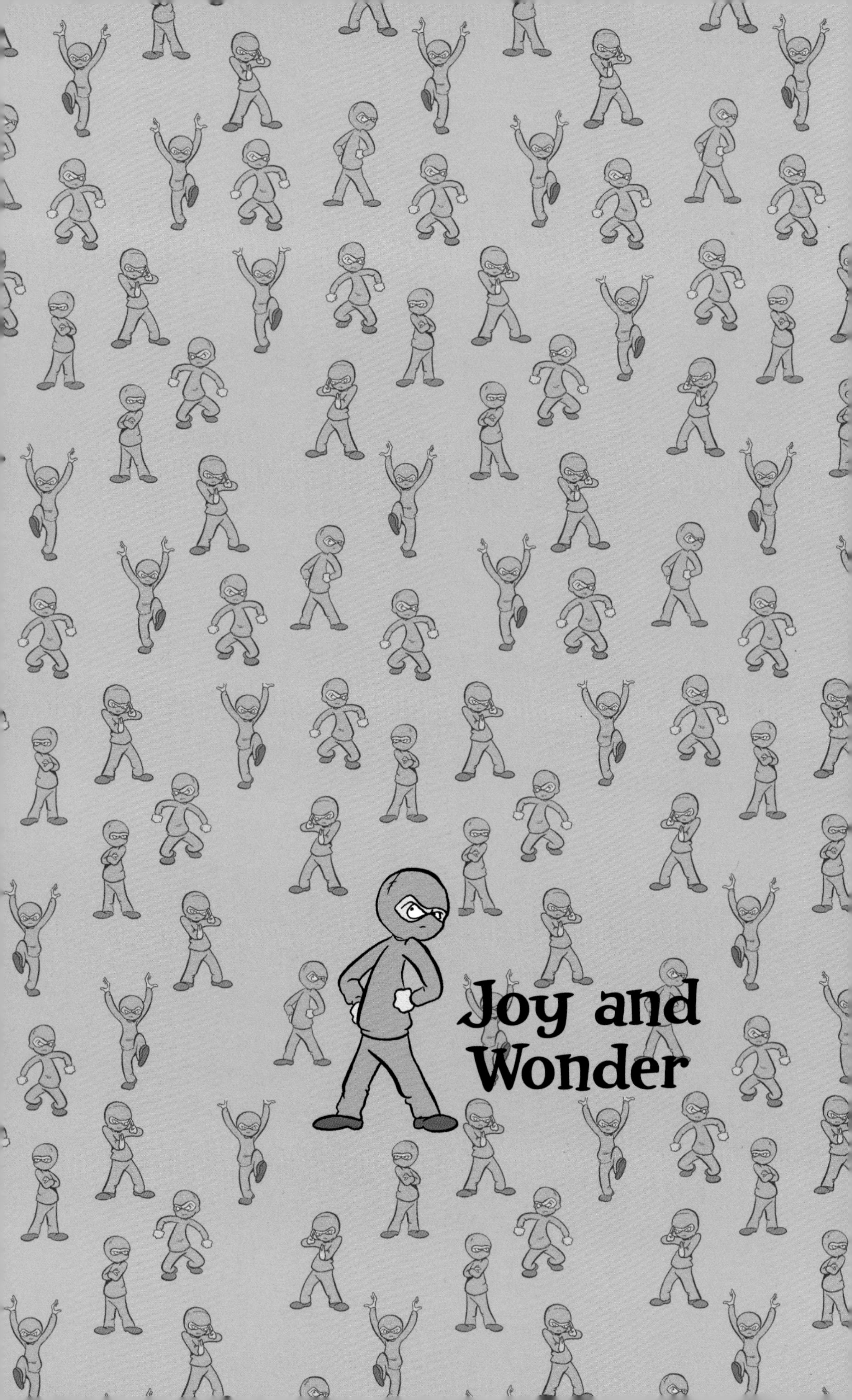

Joy and Wonder

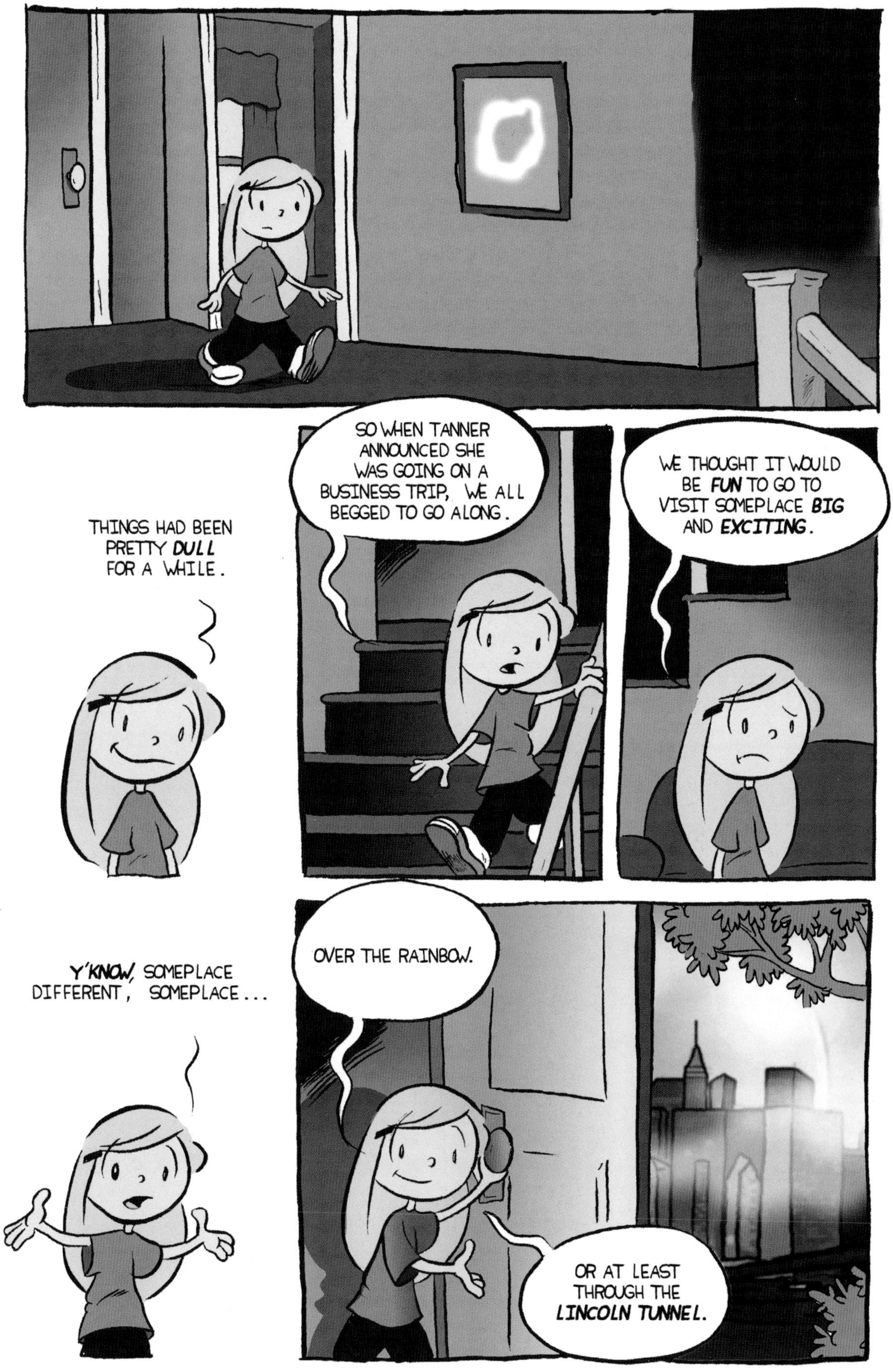
THINGS HAD BEEN PRETTY DULL FOR A WHILE.
SO WHEN TANNER ANNOUNCED SHE WAS GOING ON A BUSINESS TRIP, WE ALL BEGGED TO GO ALONG.
WE THOUGHT IT WOULD BE FUN TO GO TO VISIT SOMEPLACE BIG AND EXCITING.
Y'KNOW, SOMEPLACE DIFFERENT, SOMEPLACE...
OVER THE RAINBOW.
OR AT LEAST THROUGH THE LINCOLN TUNNEL.

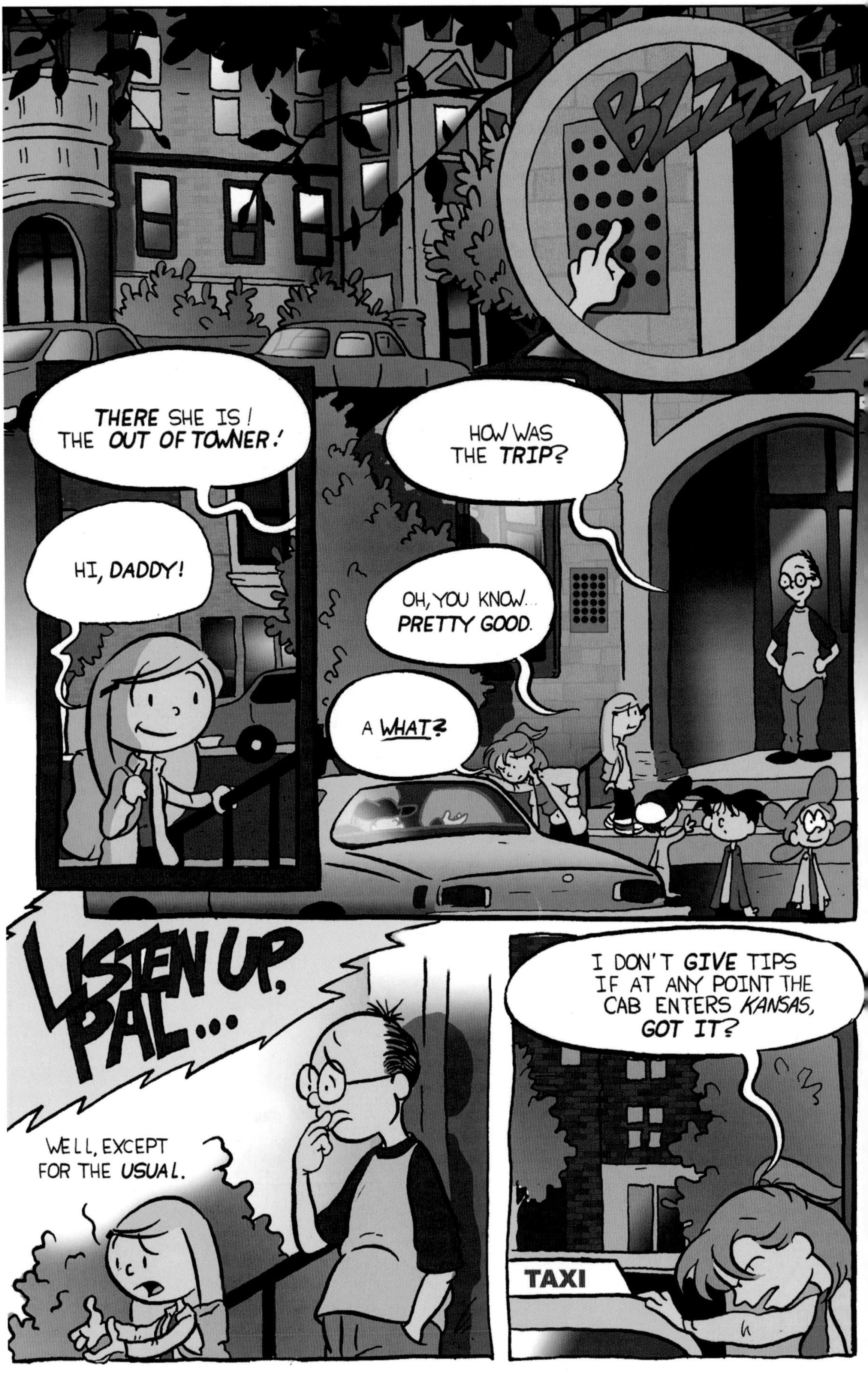
BZZZZZZ
THERE SHE IS! THE OUT OF TOWNER!
HI, DADDY!
HOW WAS THE TRIP?
OH, YOU KNOW... PRETTY GOOD.
A WHAT?
LISTEN UP, PAL...
WELL, EXCEPT FOR THE USUAL.
I DON'T GIVE TIPS IF AT ANY POINT THE CAB ENTERS KANSAS, GOT IT?
TAXI

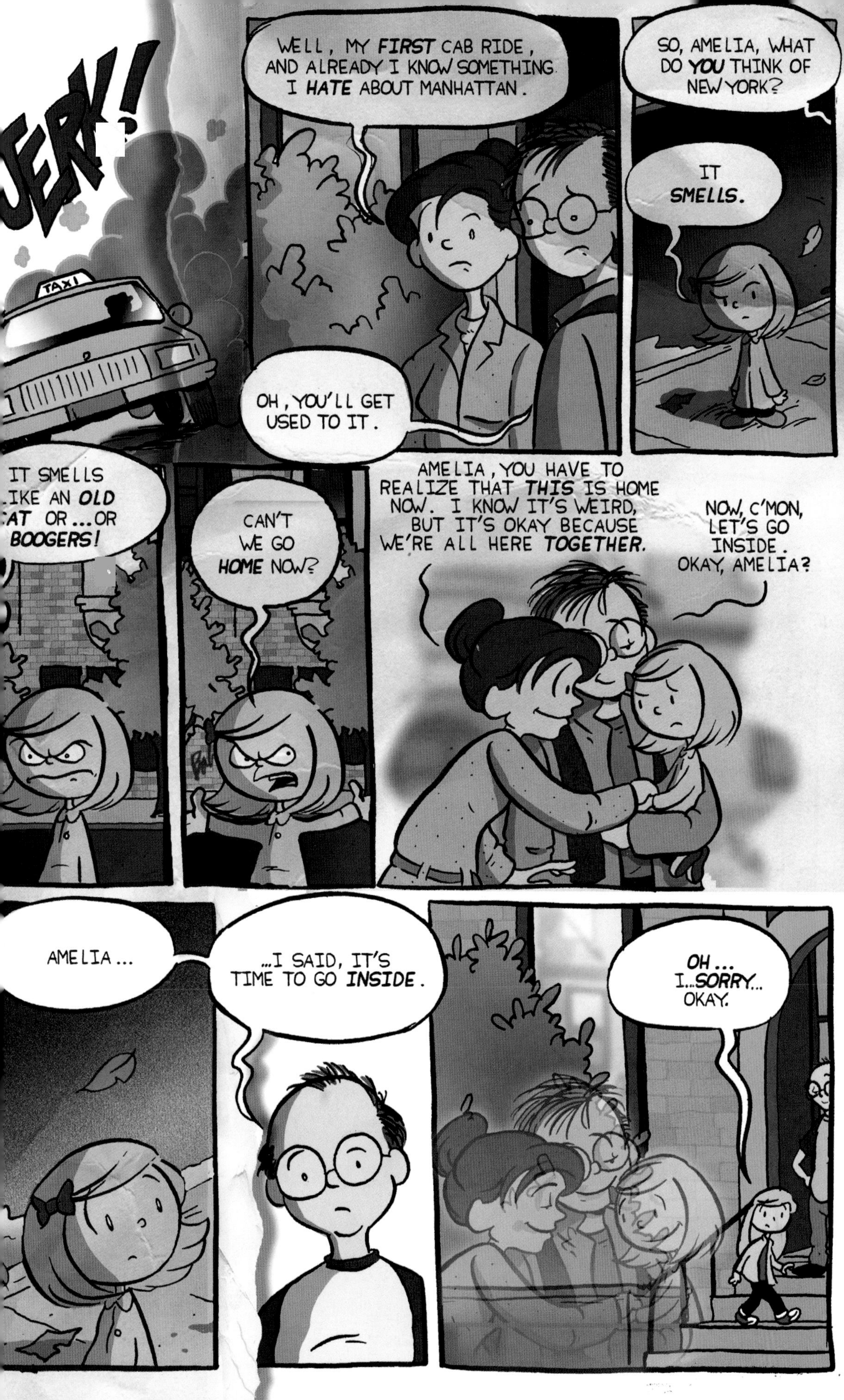
JERK!
WELL, MY FIRST CAB RIDE, AND ALREADY I KNOW SOMETHING I HATE ABOUT MANHATTAN.
OH, YOU'LL GET USED TO IT.
SO, AMELIA, WHAT DO YOU THINK OF NEW YORK?
IT SMELLS.
IT SMELLS LIKE AN OLD CAT OR...OR BOOGERS!
CAN'T WE GO HOME NOW?
AMELIA, YOU HAVE TO REALIZE THAT THIS IS HOME NOW. I KNOW IT'S WEIRD, BUT IT'S OKAY BECAUSE WE'RE ALL HERE TOGETHER.
NOW, C'MON, LET'S GO INSIDE. OKAY, AMELIA?
AMELIA...
...I SAID, IT'S TIME TO GO INSIDE.
OH... I...SORRY... OKAY.

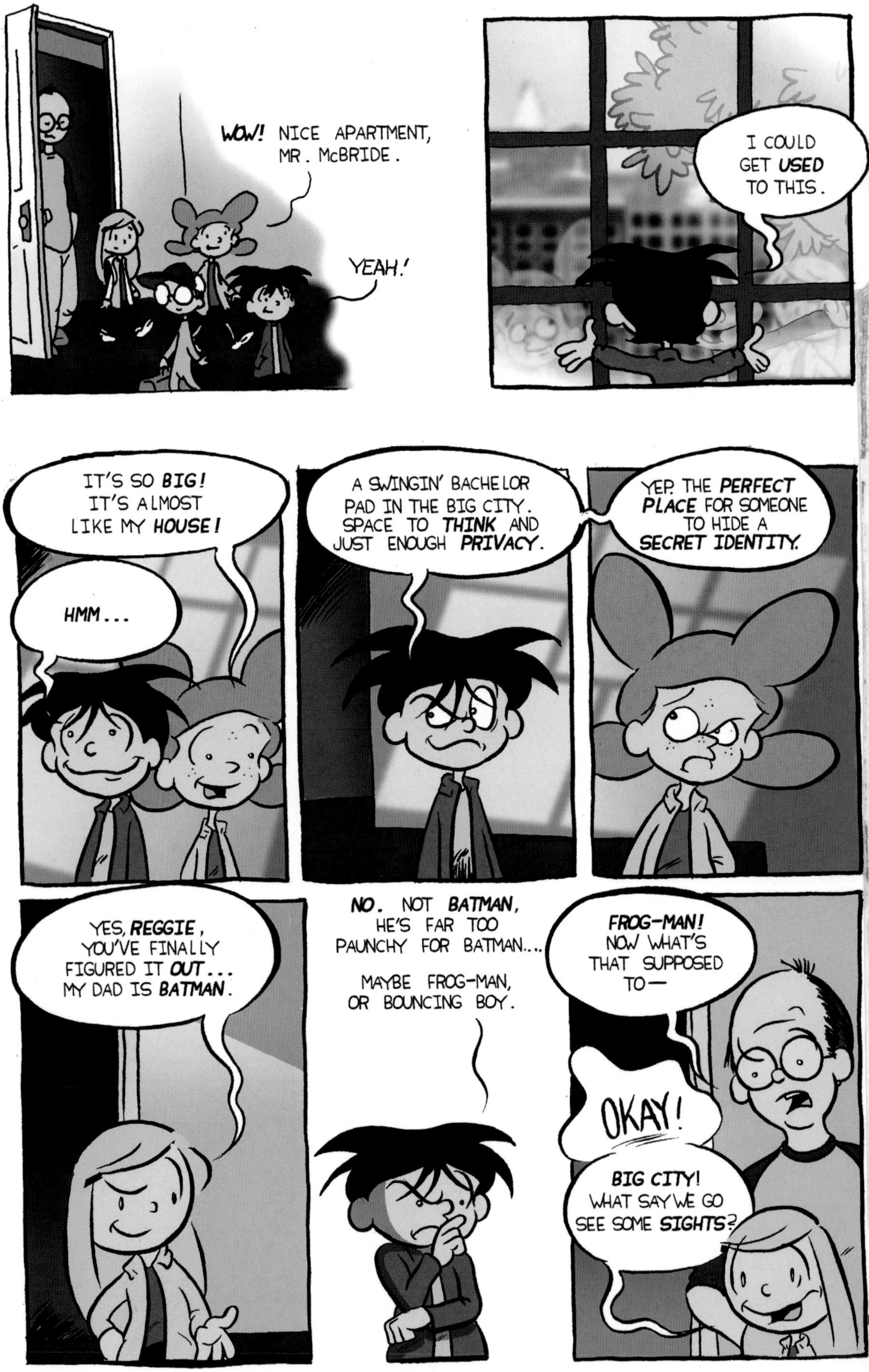
WOW! NICE APARTMENT, MR. McBRIDE.
YEAH!
I COULD GET USED TO THIS.
IT'S SO BIG! IT'S ALMOST LIKE MY HOUSE!
HMM...
A SWINGIN' BACHELOR PAD IN THE BIG CITY. SPACE TO THINK AND JUST ENOUGH PRIVACY.
YEP. THE PERFECT PLACE FOR SOMEONE TO HIDE A SECRET IDENTITY.
YES, REGGIE, YOU'VE FINALLY FIGURED IT OUT... MY DAD IS BATMAN.
NO. NOT BATMAN, HE'S FAR TOO PAUNCHY FOR BATMAN....
MAYBE FROG-MAN, OR BOUNCING BOY.
FROG-MAN! NOW WHAT'S THAT SUPPOSED TO—
OKAY!
BIG CITY! WHAT SAY WE GO SEE SOME SIGHTS?

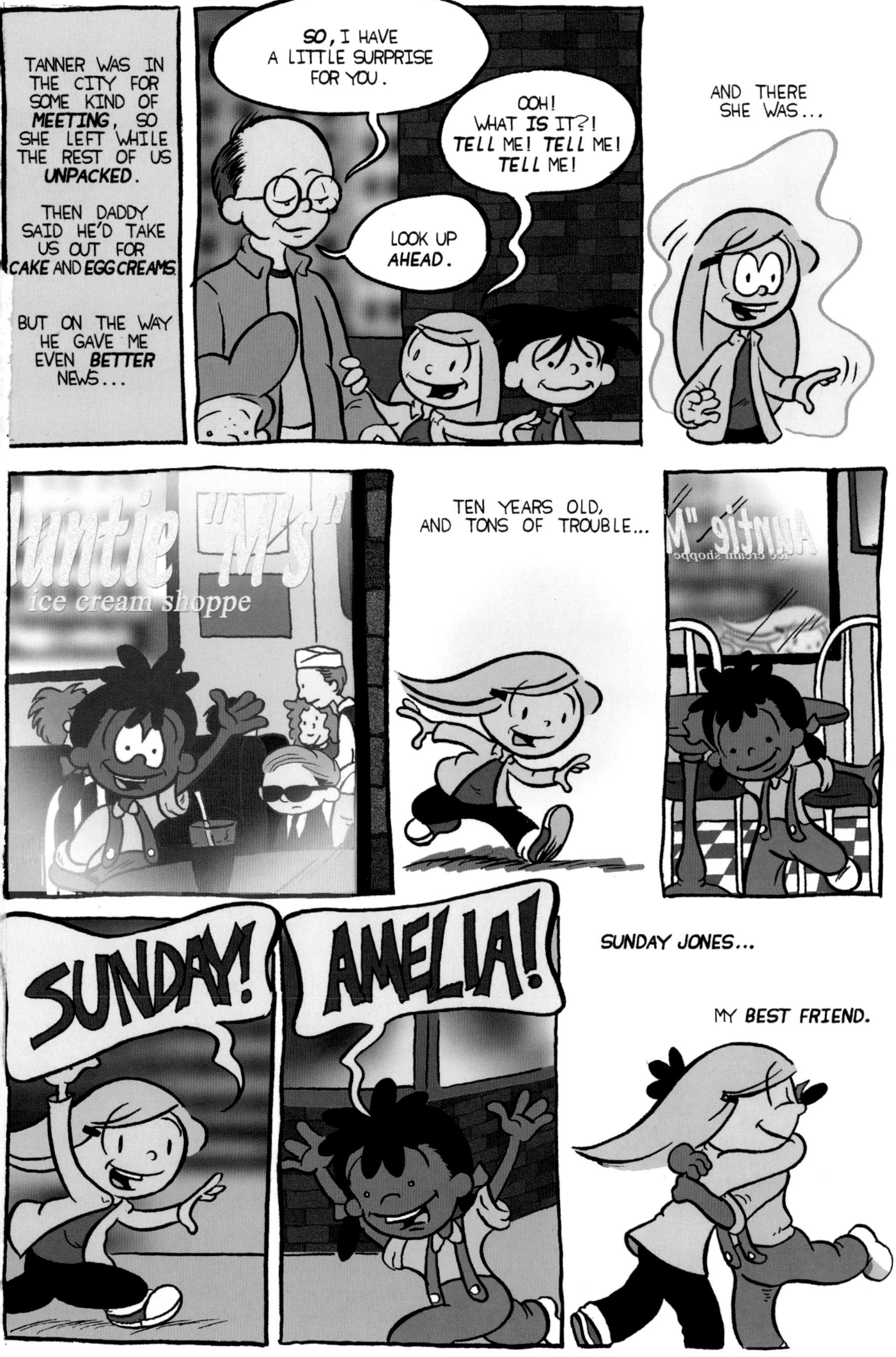
TANNER WAS IN THE CITY FOR SOME KIND OF MEETING, SO SHE LEFT WHILE THE REST OF US UNPACKED.
THEN DADDY SAID HE'D TAKE US OUT FOR CAKE AND EGG CREAMS.
BUT ON THE WAY HE GAVE ME EVEN BETTER NEWS...
SO, I HAVE A LITTLE SURPRISE FOR YOU.
OOH! WHAT IS IT?! TELL ME! TELL ME! TELL ME!
LOOK UP AHEAD.
AND THERE SHE WAS...
ice cream shoppe
TEN YEARS OLD, AND TONS OF TROUBLE...
ice cream shoppe
SUNDAY!
AMELIA!
SUNDAY JONES...
MY BEST FRIEND.

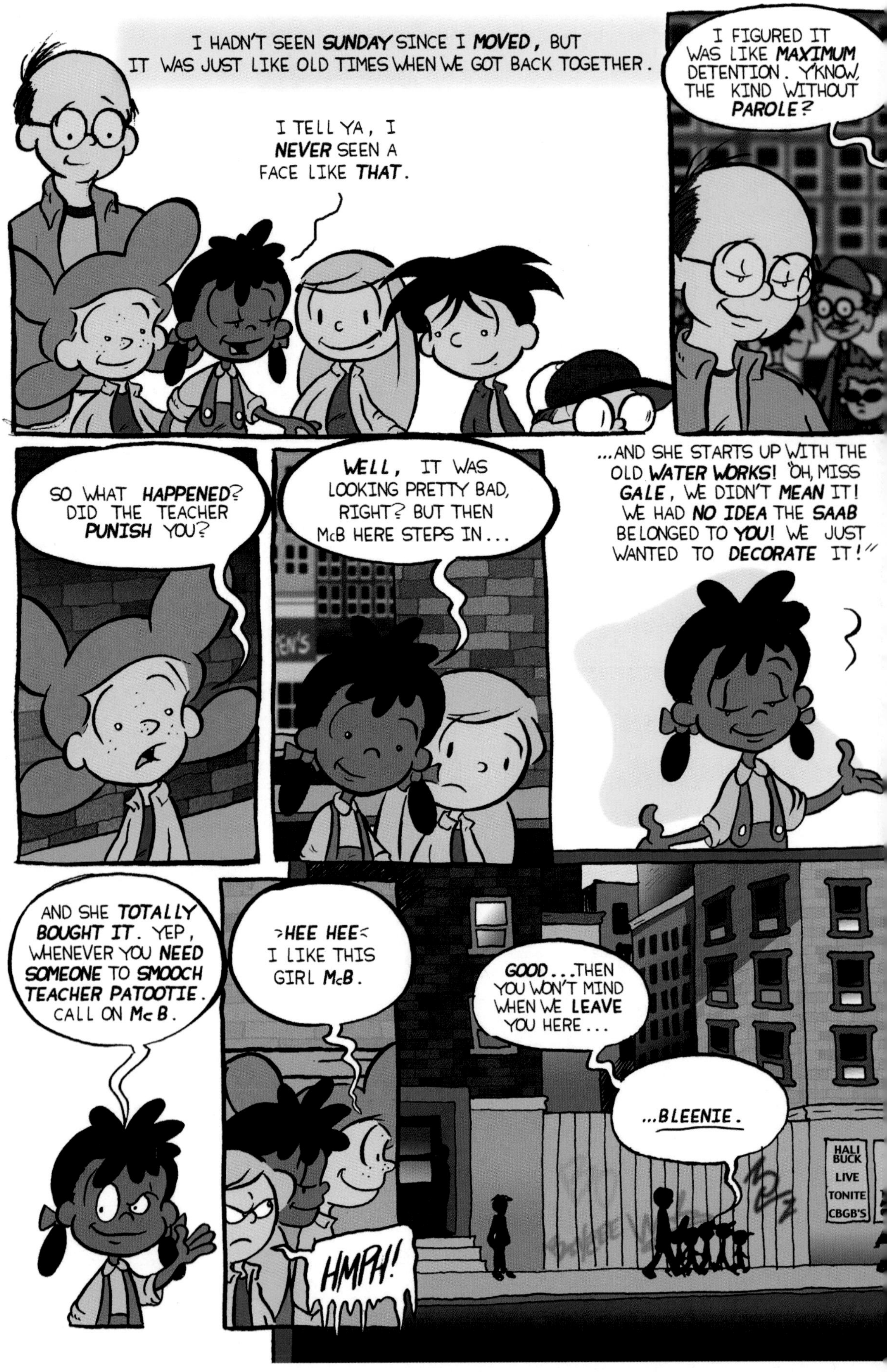
I HADN'T SEEN SUNDAY SINCE I MOVED, BUT IT WAS JUST LIKE OLD TIMES WHEN WE GOT BACK TOGETHER.
I TELL YA, I NEVER SEEN A FACE LIKE THAT.
I FIGURED IT WAS LIKE MAXIMUM DETENTION. Y'KNOW, THE KIND WITHOUT PAROLE?
SO WHAT HAPPENED? DID THE TEACHER PUNISH YOU?
WELL, IT WAS LOOKING PRETTY BAD, RIGHT? BUT THEN McB HERE STEPS IN...
...AND SHE STARTS UP WITH THE OLD WATER WORKS! "OH, MISS GALE, WE DIDN'T MEAN IT! WE HAD NO IDEA THE SAAB BELONGED TO YOU! WE JUST WANTED TO DECORATE IT!"
AND SHE TOTALLY BOUGHT IT. YEP, WHENEVER YOU NEED SOMEONE TO SMOOCH TEACHER PATOOTIE, CALL ON McB.
>HEE HEE< I LIKE THIS GIRL McB.
HMPH!
GOOD...THEN YOU WON'T MIND WHEN WE LEAVE YOU HERE...
...BLEENIE.
HALI BUCK LIVE TONITE CBGB'S

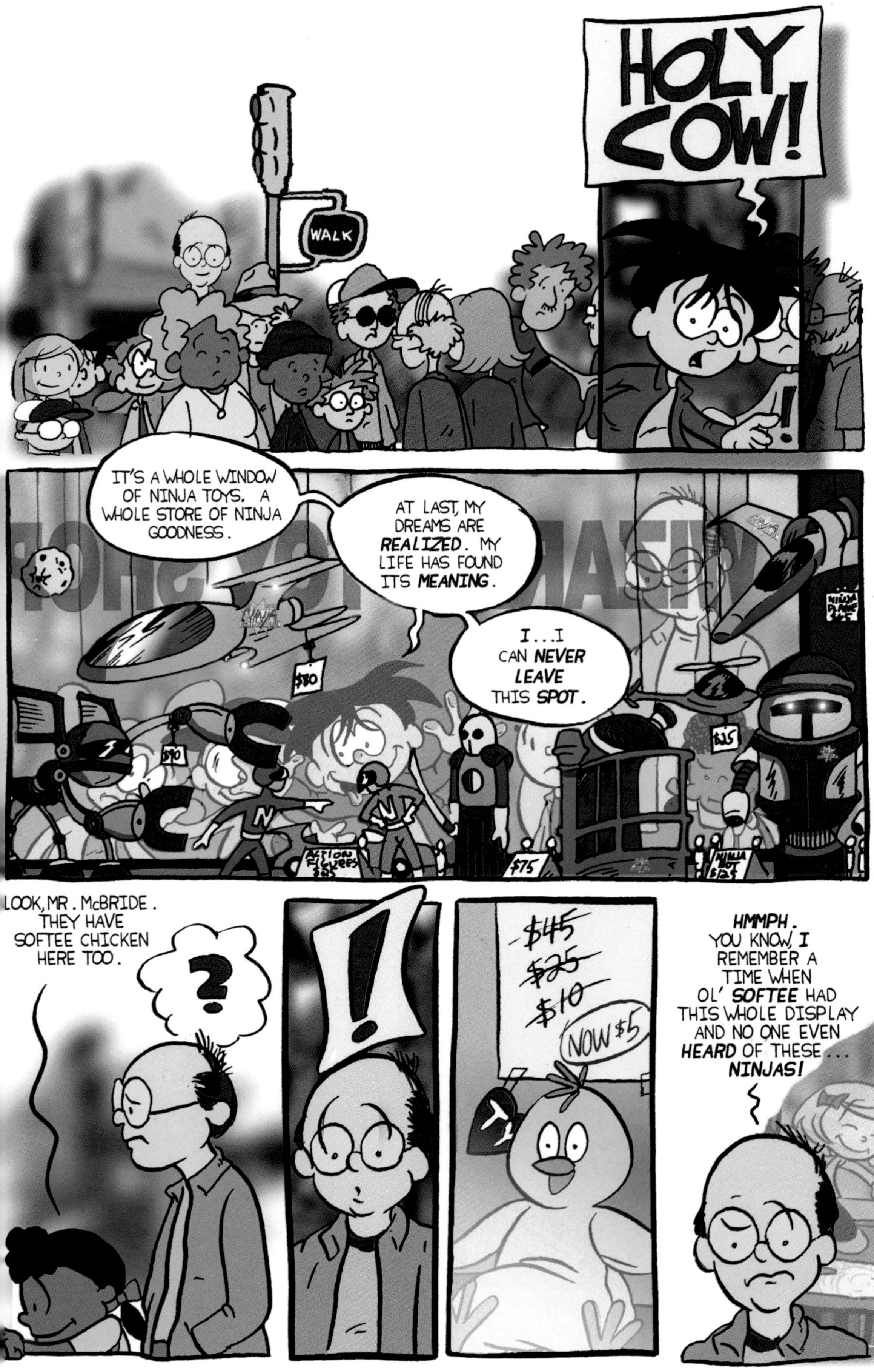
WALK
HOLY COW!
IT'S A WHOLE WINDOW OF NINJA TOYS. A WHOLE STORE OF NINJA GOODNESS.
AT LAST, MY DREAMS ARE REALIZED. MY LIFE HAS FOUND ITS MEANING.
I...I CAN NEVER LEAVE THIS SPOT.
$80
$90
$75
ACTION FIGURES
LOOK, MR. McBRIDE. THEY HAVE SOFTEE CHICKEN HERE TOO.
?
!
$45 $25 $10 NOW $5
HMMPH. YOU KNOW, I REMEMBER A TIME WHEN OL' SOFTEE HAD THIS WHOLE DISPLAY AND NO ONE EVEN HEARD OF THESE... NINJAS!

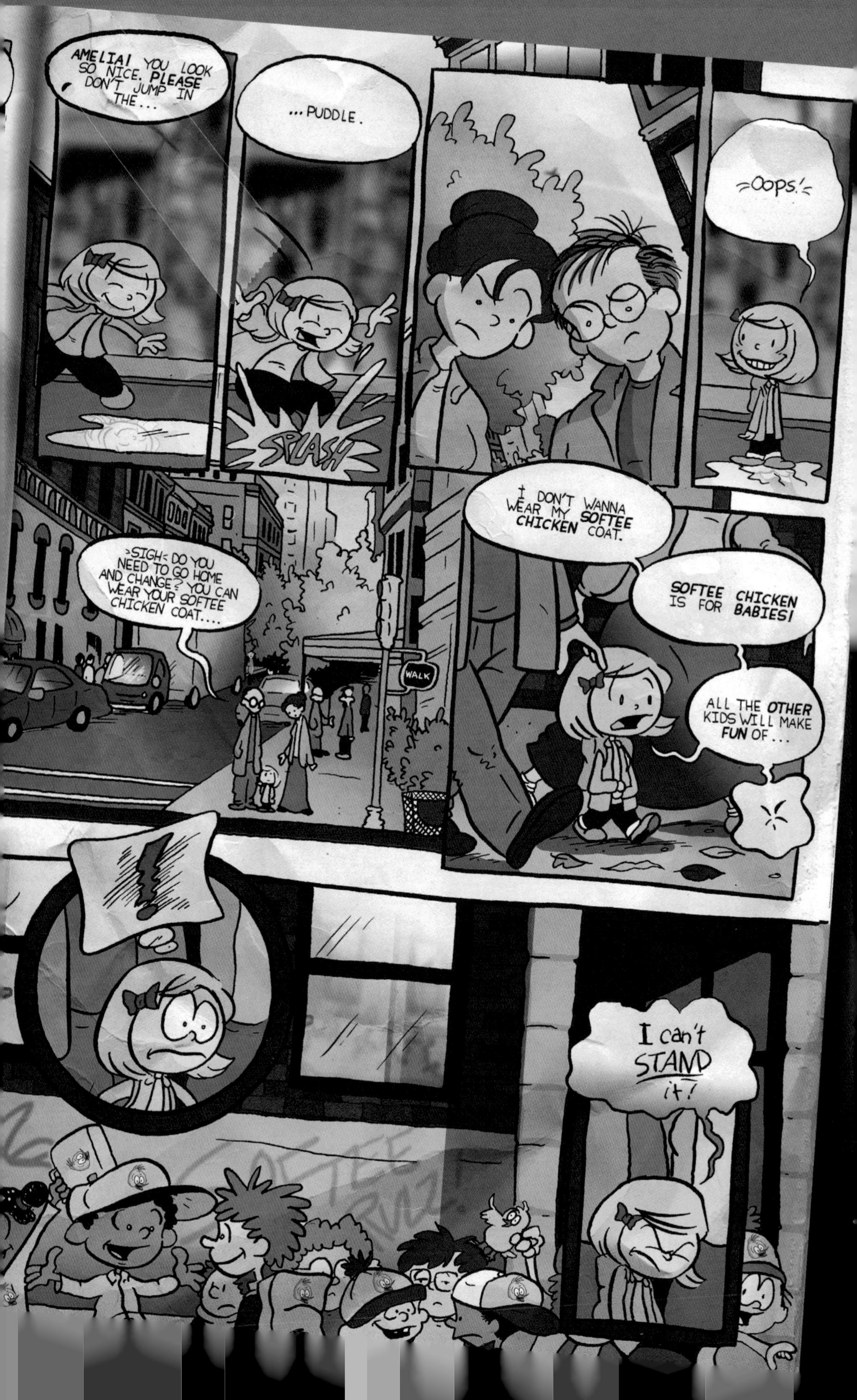
AMELIA! YOU LOOK SO NICE. PLEASE DON'T JUMP IN THE...
...PUDDLE.
SPLASH
=Oops!=
>SIGH< DO YOU NEED TO GO HOME AND CHANGE? YOU CAN WEAR YOUR SOFTEE CHICKEN COAT....
WALK
I DON'T WANNA WEAR MY SOFTEE CHICKEN COAT.
SOFTEE CHICKEN IS FOR BABIES!
ALL THE OTHER KIDS WILL MAKE FUN OF...
!
I can't STAND it!

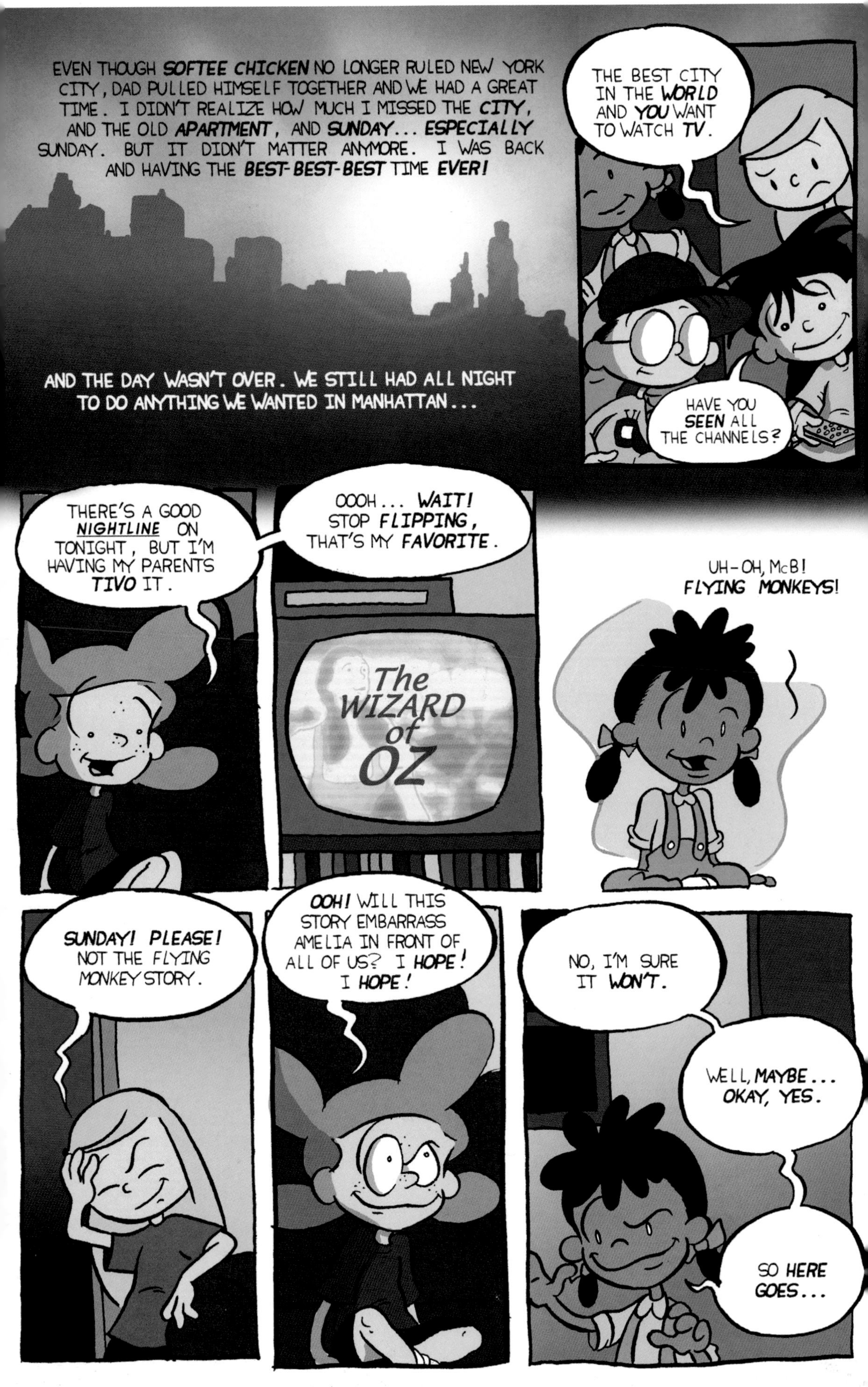
EVEN THOUGH SOFTEE CHICKEN NO LONGER RULED NEW YORK CITY, DAD PULLED HIMSELF TOGETHER AND WE HAD A GREAT TIME. I DIDN'T REALIZE HOW MUCH I MISSED THE CITY, AND THE OLD APARTMENT, AND SUNDAY... ESPECIALLY SUNDAY. BUT IT DIDN'T MATTER ANYMORE. I WAS BACK AND HAVING THE BEST-BEST-BEST TIME EVER!
AND THE DAY WASN'T OVER. WE STILL HAD ALL NIGHT TO DO ANYTHING WE WANTED IN MANHATTAN...
THE BEST CITY IN THE WORLD AND YOU WANT TO WATCH TV.
HAVE YOU SEEN ALL THE CHANNELS?
THERE'S A GOOD NIGHTLINE ON TONIGHT, BUT I'M HAVING MY PARENTS TIVO IT.
OOOH... WAIT! STOP FLIPPING, THAT'S MY FAVORITE.
The WIZARD of OZ
UH-OH, McB! FLYING MONKEYS!
SUNDAY! PLEASE! NOT THE FLYING MONKEY STORY.
OOH! WILL THIS STORY EMBARRASS AMELIA IN FRONT OF ALL OF US? I HOPE! I HOPE!
NO, I'M SURE IT WON'T.
WELL, MAYBE... OKAY, YES.
SO HERE GOES...

It was back in first grade. See, by the time McB came to town, school had already been rolling for a while. And let's just say I had already made my rep. What I hadn't made was, y'know, any friends. And on top of that, we had this teacher, Miss Hamilton. She was a real witch, and she had it in for me BIG TIME.

And, really, it was for no reason. I mean, sure, there were one or two little things, but the fire department was barely involved. And besides, they couldn't prove anyth–

Uh...anyway...

So when Amelia joined the class, I barely even noticed. She was just this quiet, shy girl who kept to herself, and...

Rhonda?
Rhonda? What's so funny? Are you okay? Breathe, girl! ***BREATHE!***

So like I said, I pretty much ignored her. Then one day I noticed something.

If there was one person Miss Hamilton liked less than me, it was Amelia Louise McBride.

See, that's even what she called her... Amelia Louise... Never just Amelia, she always stuck on Louise. Only it sounded like this...

Leweeeeeeeeeeez.

Like she just stepped in something nasty.

Rhonda, if you can't control the laughing, we'll have to ask you to leave.

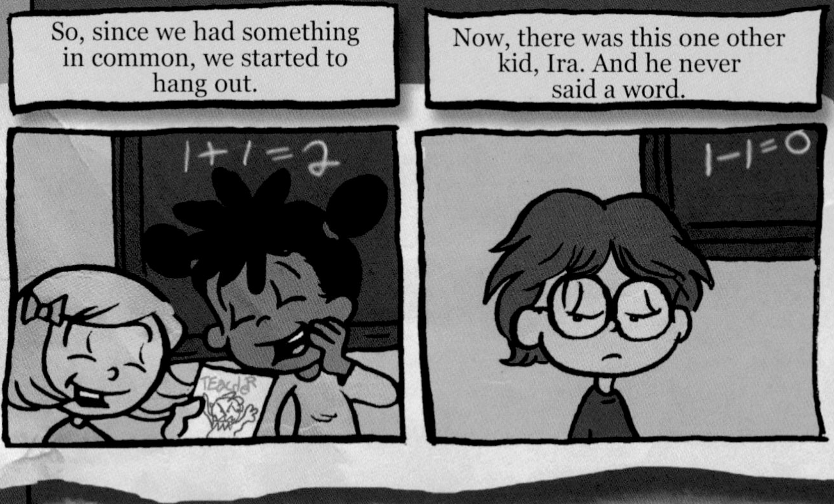
So, since we had something in common, we started to hang out.
1+1=2
Now, there was this one other kid, Ira. And he never said a word.
1-1=0

Can you imagine that? A kid who went all day without ever saying...oh... yeah...I guess you can. Anyway, it seemed like the three of us were invisible to the rest of the class.

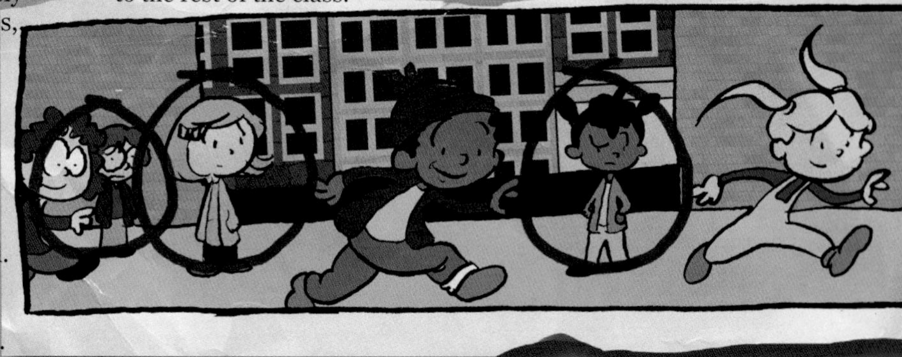

One day Miss Hamilton says the class is gonna do a play, the ***Wizard of Oz***, right? So everyone gets real excited, and she starts handin' out the parts.

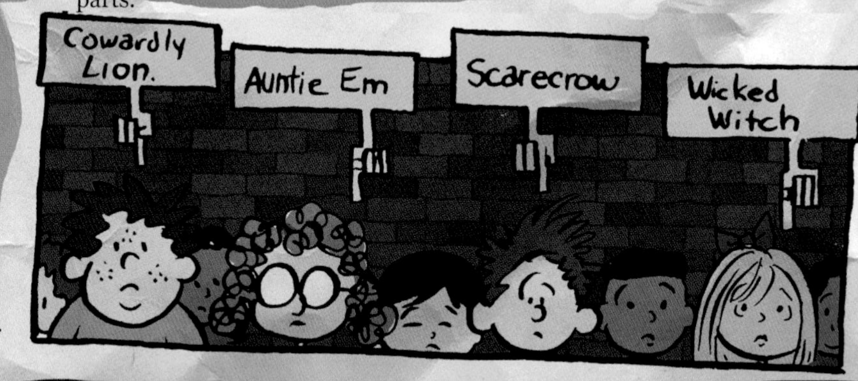
Cowardly Lion.
Auntie Em
Scarecrow
Wicked Witch

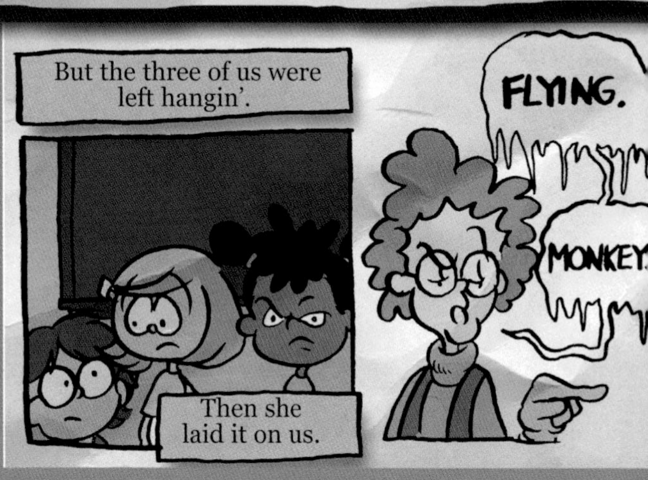
But the three of us were left hangin'.
FLYING.
MONKEYS.
Then she laid it on us.

Not exactly a compliment, y'know? I mean, it's not like she picked her favorite students and said, "Ah, yes...You shall be my monkeys." It was more like, "Let's put these numbskulls where they can do the least amount of damage."

I think Mr. and Mrs. McBride felt bad for us. They invited us over a bunch of times so we could "rehearse" with Amelia. Not that there was much to rehearse. We pretty much just ran around the apartment going, "Eek! Eek!" But, y'know, it was fun.

The best part was when Amelia's mom made us these way cool monkey costumes. They had wings and ears and big ol' monkey tails. We were stylin'! I think that's when we started getting into it. I came up with this name, "The Flying Monkey Society," and we ran around calling ourselves that. Whenever someone would ask what time it was, we'd yell, "IT'S MONKEY TIME!" (Well, me and McB would. Ira still wasn't talking) and then we'd jump around like rejects.

It must've looked like fun, cuz pretty soon everyone wanted to be a Flying Monkey. Of course, we wouldn't let them. Heh, heh...It was pretty cool.

So, anyway, the day of the big show finally comes, and everyone is freaking out. Even Miss Hamilton is kinda goin' wonky. And the more wonky she got, the more freaked out we got. It was a scene.

Then things really went downhill. First, the girl who was playing Dorothy forgot the words to "Somewhere Over the Rainbow." Then the Tin Man got the hiccups, which wouldn't have been so bad if it didn't make Carlos, the kid playing the Scarecrow, laugh. He laughed so hard he fell off the stage. By the time we came on, it was a massacre. People were leaving. I'm pretty sure I even heard another teacher boo us.

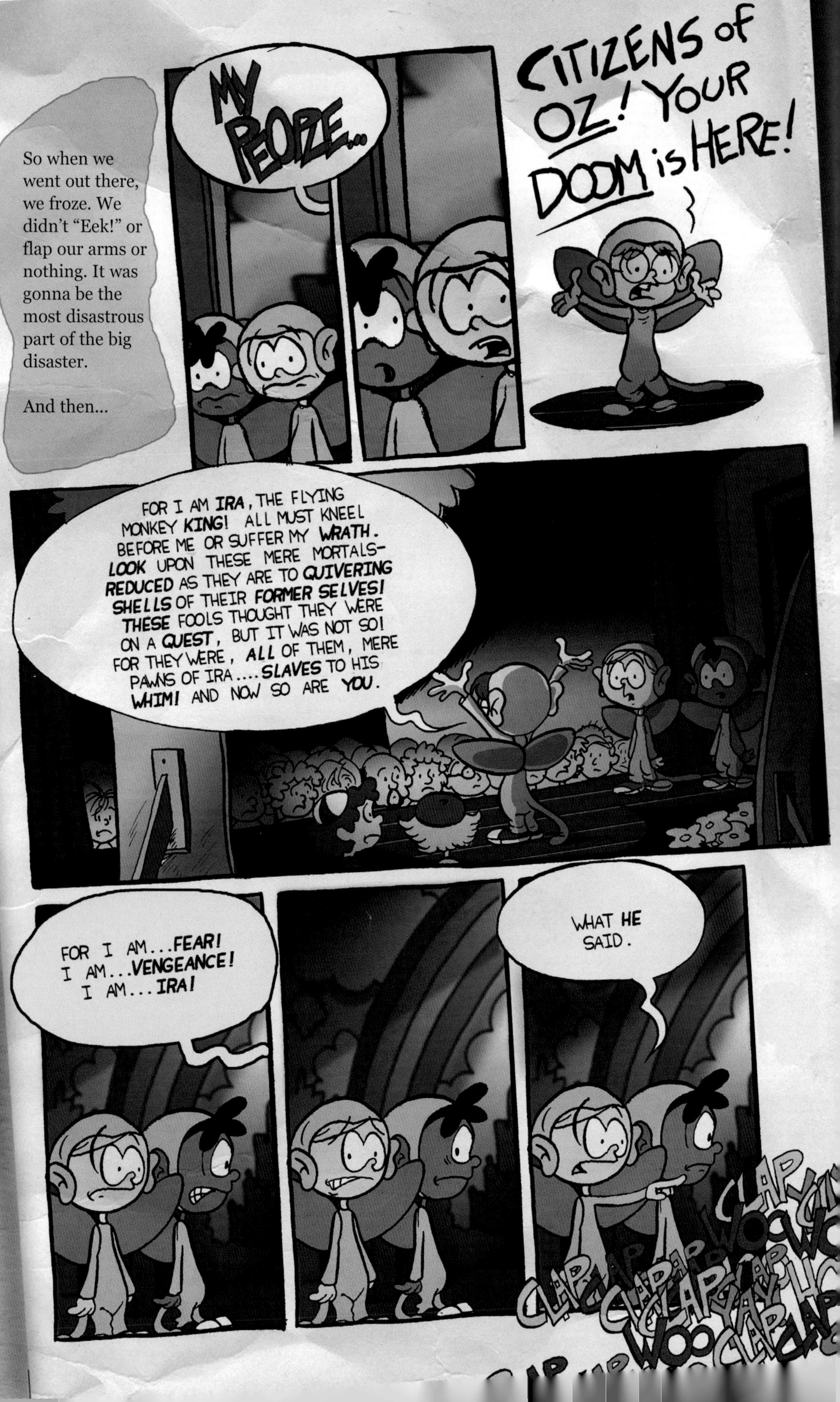
So when we went out there, we froze. We didn't "Eek!" or flap our arms or nothing. It was gonna be the most disastrous part of the big disaster.
And then...
MY PEOPLE...
CITIZENS of OZ! YOUR DOOM is HERE!
FOR I AM IRA, THE FLYING MONKEY KING! ALL MUST KNEEL BEFORE ME OR SUFFER MY WRATH. LOOK UPON THESE MERE MORTALS- REDUCED AS THEY ARE TO QUIVERING SHELLS OF THEIR FORMER SELVES! THESE FOOLS THOUGHT THEY WERE ON A QUEST, BUT IT WAS NOT SO! FOR THEY WERE, ALL OF THEM, MERE PAWNS OF IRA.... SLAVES TO HIS WHIM! AND NOW SO ARE YOU.
FOR I AM...FEAR! I AM...VENGEANCE! I AM...IRA!
WHAT HE SAID.
CLAP CLAP WOO CLAP CLAP WOO CLAP

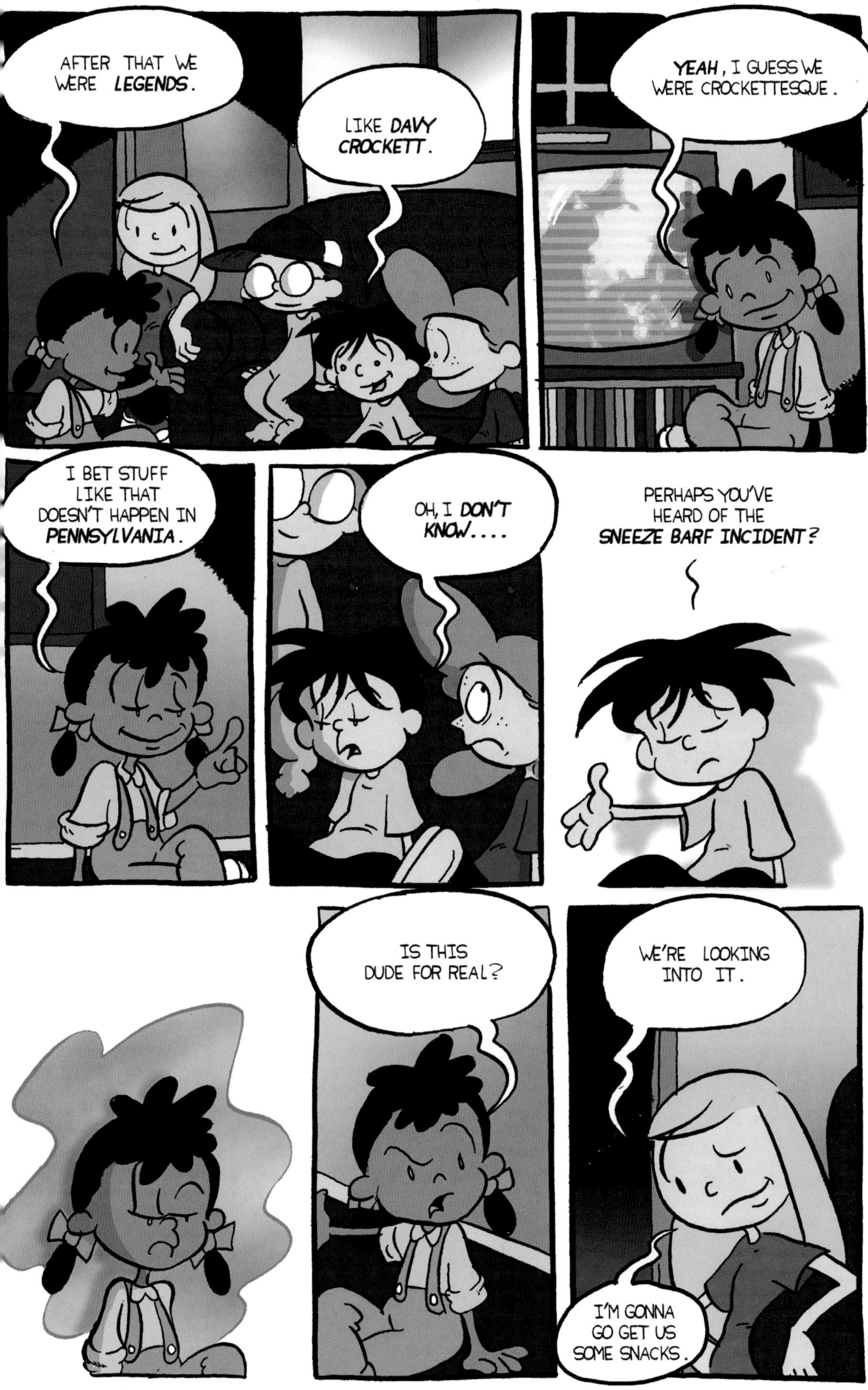
AFTER THAT WE WERE LEGENDS.
LIKE DAVY CROCKETT.
YEAH, I GUESS WE WERE CROCKETTESQUE.
I BET STUFF LIKE THAT DOESN'T HAPPEN IN PENNSYLVANIA.
OH, I DON'T KNOW....
PERHAPS YOU'VE HEARD OF THE SNEEZE BARF INCIDENT?
IS THIS DUDE FOR REAL?
WE'RE LOOKING INTO IT.
I'M GONNA GO GET US SOME SNACKS.

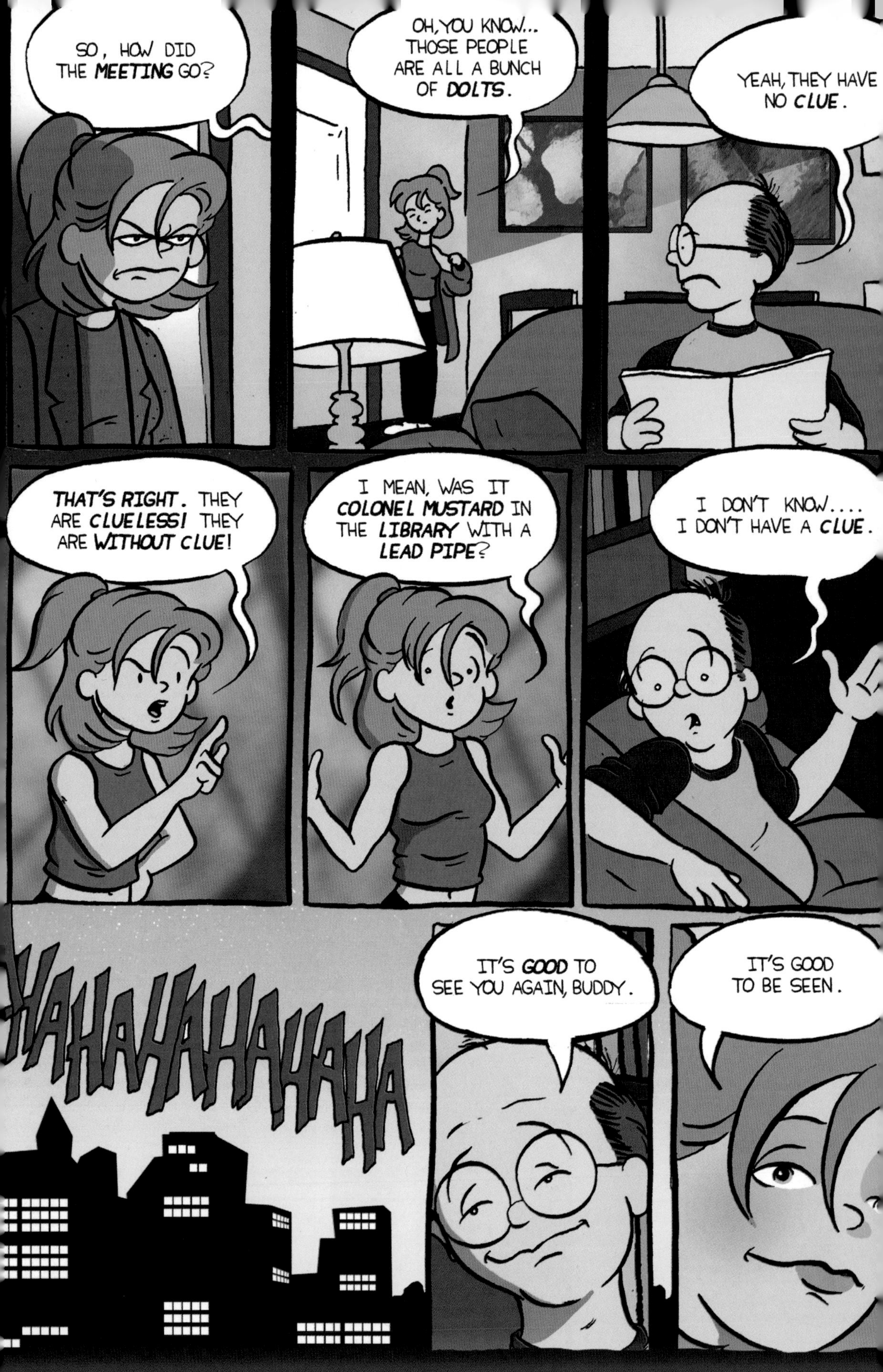
SO, HOW DID THE MEETING GO?
OH, YOU KNOW... THOSE PEOPLE ARE ALL A BUNCH OF DOLTS.
YEAH, THEY HAVE NO CLUE.
THAT'S RIGHT. THEY ARE CLUELESS! THEY ARE WITHOUT CLUE!
I MEAN, WAS IT COLONEL MUSTARD IN THE LIBRARY WITH A LEAD PIPE?
I DON'T KNOW.... I DON'T HAVE A CLUE.
HAHAHAHAHAHAHA
IT'S GOOD TO SEE YOU AGAIN, BUDDY.
IT'S GOOD TO BE SEEN.

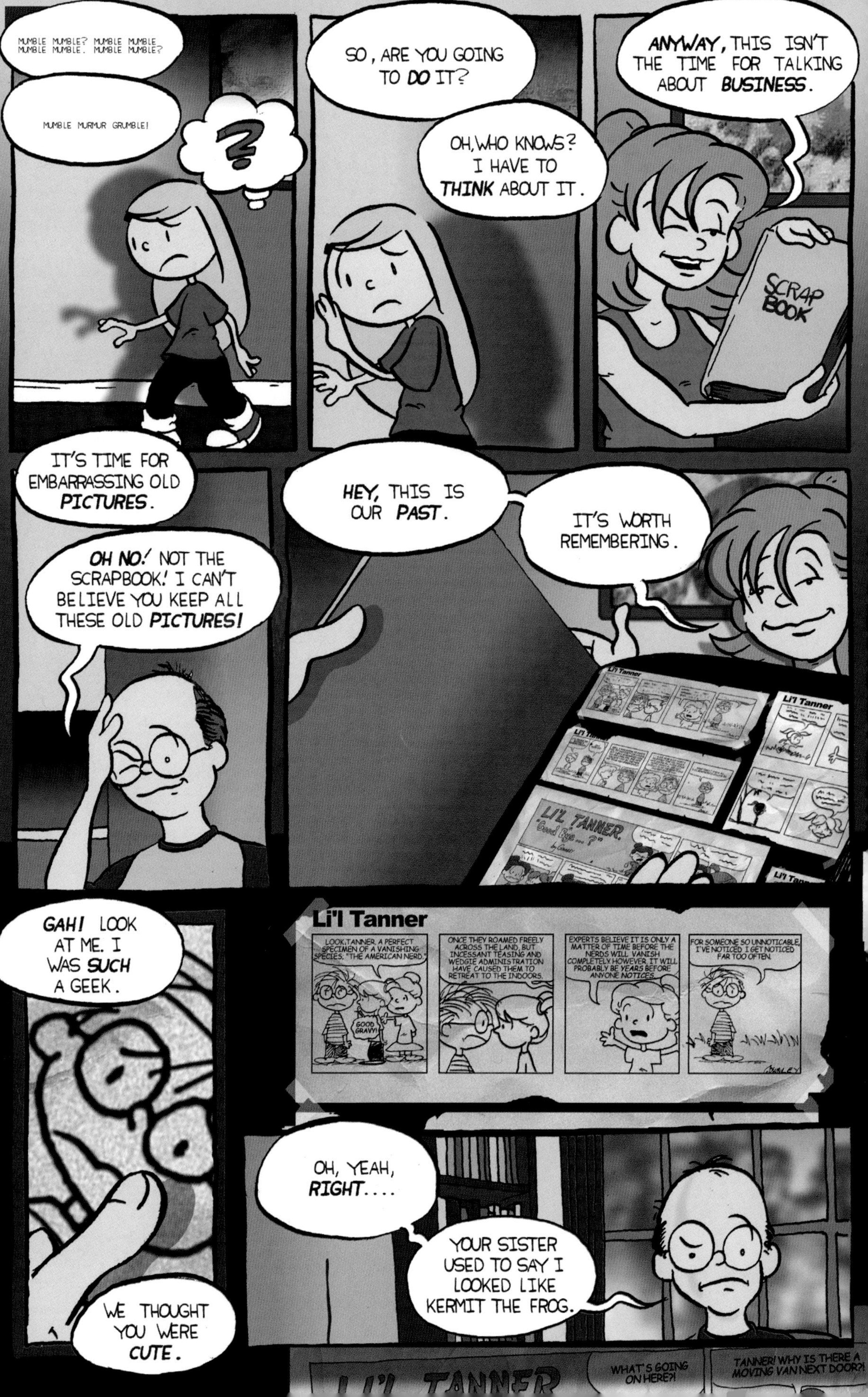
MUMBLE MUMBLE? MUMBLE MUMBLE. MUMBLE MUMBLE. MUMBLE MUMBLE?
MUMBLE MURMUR GRUMBLE!
?
SO, ARE YOU GOING TO **DO** IT?
OH, WHO KNOWS? I HAVE TO **THINK** ABOUT IT.
ANYWAY, THIS ISN'T THE TIME FOR TALKING ABOUT **BUSINESS**.
SCRAP BOOK
IT'S TIME FOR EMBARRASSING OLD **PICTURES**.
OH NO! NOT THE SCRAPBOOK! I CAN'T BELIEVE YOU KEEP ALL THESE OLD **PICTURES!**
HEY, THIS IS OUR **PAST**.
IT'S WORTH REMEMBERING.
Li'l Tanner
LI'L TANNER
"Good Bye...?"
GAH! LOOK AT ME. I WAS **SUCH** A GEEK.
Li'l Tanner
LOOK, TANNER. A PERFECT SPECIMEN OF A VANISHING SPECIES: "THE AMERICAN NERD."
GOOD GRAVY!
ONCE THEY ROAMED FREELY ACROSS THE LAND, BUT INCESSANT TEASING AND WEDGIE ADMINISTRATION HAVE CAUSED THEM TO RETREAT TO THE INDOORS.
EXPERTS BELIEVE IT IS ONLY A MATTER OF TIME BEFORE THE NERDS WILL VANISH COMPLETELY. HOWEVER, IT WILL PROBABLY BE *YEARS* BEFORE ANYONE *NOTICES*.
FOR SOMEONE SO UNNOTICABLE, I'VE NOTICED I GET NOTICED FAR TOO OFTEN.
WE THOUGHT YOU WERE **CUTE**.
OH, YEAH, **RIGHT**....
YOUR SISTER USED TO SAY I LOOKED LIKE KERMIT THE FROG.
LI'L TANNER
WHAT'S GOING ON HERE?!
TANNER! WHY IS THERE A MOVING VAN NEXT DOOR?!

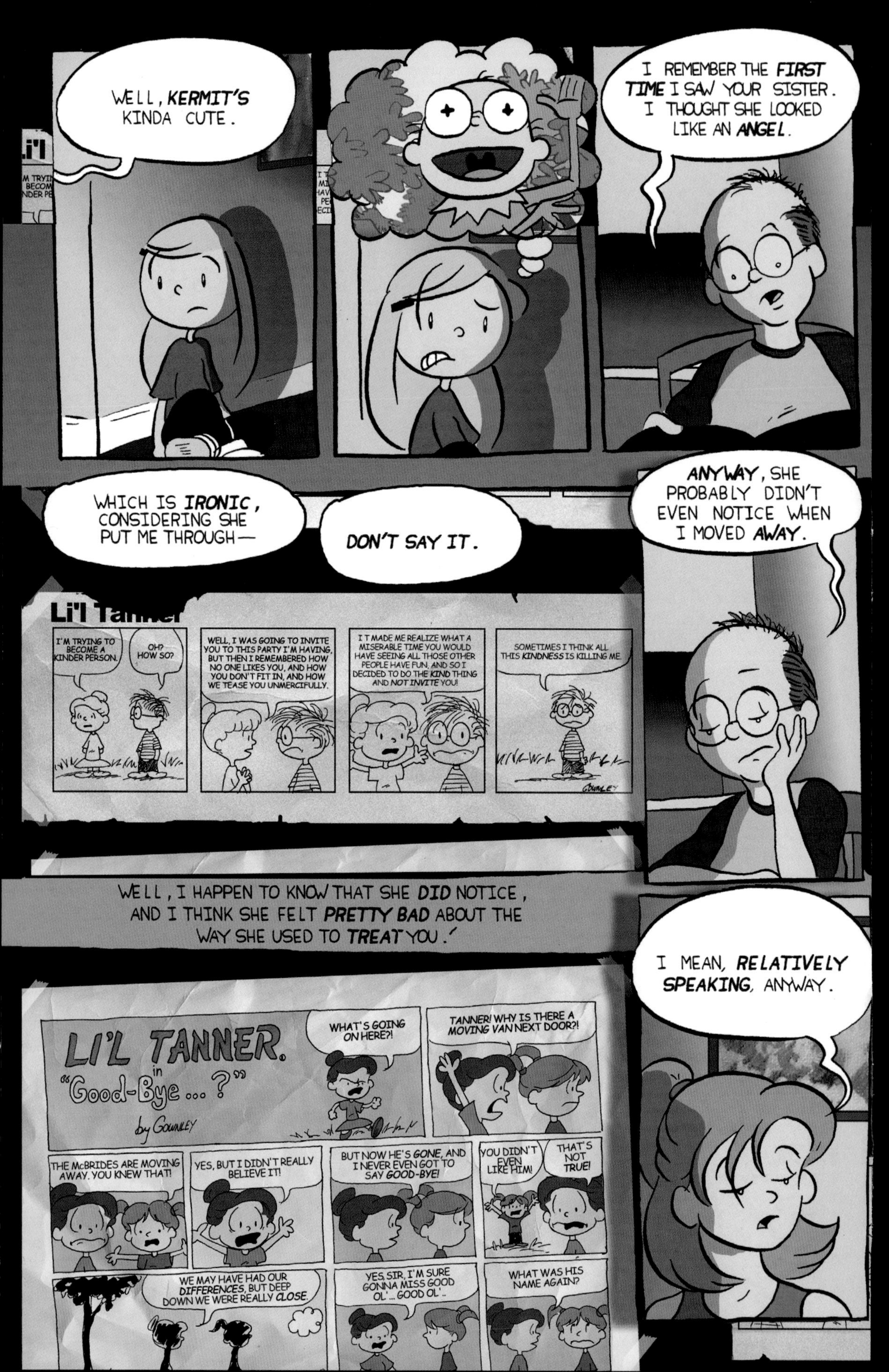
WELL, KERMIT'S KINDA CUTE.
I REMEMBER THE FIRST TIME I SAW YOUR SISTER. I THOUGHT SHE LOOKED LIKE AN ANGEL.
WHICH IS IRONIC, CONSIDERING SHE PUT ME THROUGH—
DON'T SAY IT.
ANYWAY, SHE PROBABLY DIDN'T EVEN NOTICE WHEN I MOVED AWAY.
Li'l Tanner
I'M TRYING TO BECOME A KINDER PERSON.
OH? HOW SO?
WELL, I WAS GOING TO INVITE YOU TO THIS PARTY I'M HAVING, BUT THEN I REMEMBERED HOW NO ONE LIKES YOU, AND HOW YOU DON'T FIT IN, AND HOW WE TEASE YOU UNMERCIFULLY.
IT MADE ME REALIZE WHAT A MISERABLE TIME YOU WOULD HAVE SEEING ALL THOSE OTHER PEOPLE HAVE FUN, AND SO I DECIDED TO DO THE KIND THING AND NOT INVITE YOU!
SOMETIMES I THINK ALL THIS KINDNESS IS KILLING ME.
GOUNLEY
WELL, I HAPPEN TO KNOW THAT SHE DID NOTICE, AND I THINK SHE FELT PRETTY BAD ABOUT THE WAY SHE USED TO TREAT YOU.
I MEAN, RELATIVELY SPEAKING, ANYWAY.
LI'L TANNER. in "Good-Bye ... ?" by GOUNLEY
WHAT'S GOING ON HERE?!
TANNER! WHY IS THERE A MOVING VAN NEXT DOOR?!
THE McBRIDES ARE MOVING AWAY. YOU KNEW THAT!
YES, BUT I DIDN'T REALLY BELIEVE IT!
BUT NOW HE'S GONE, AND I NEVER EVEN GOT TO SAY GOOD-BYE!
YOU DIDN'T EVEN LIKE HIM!
THAT'S NOT TRUE!
WE MAY HAVE HAD OUR DIFFERENCES, BUT DEEP DOWN WE WERE REALLY CLOSE.
YES, SIR, I'M SURE GONNA MISS GOOD OL'... GOOD OL'..
WHAT WAS HIS NAME AGAIN?

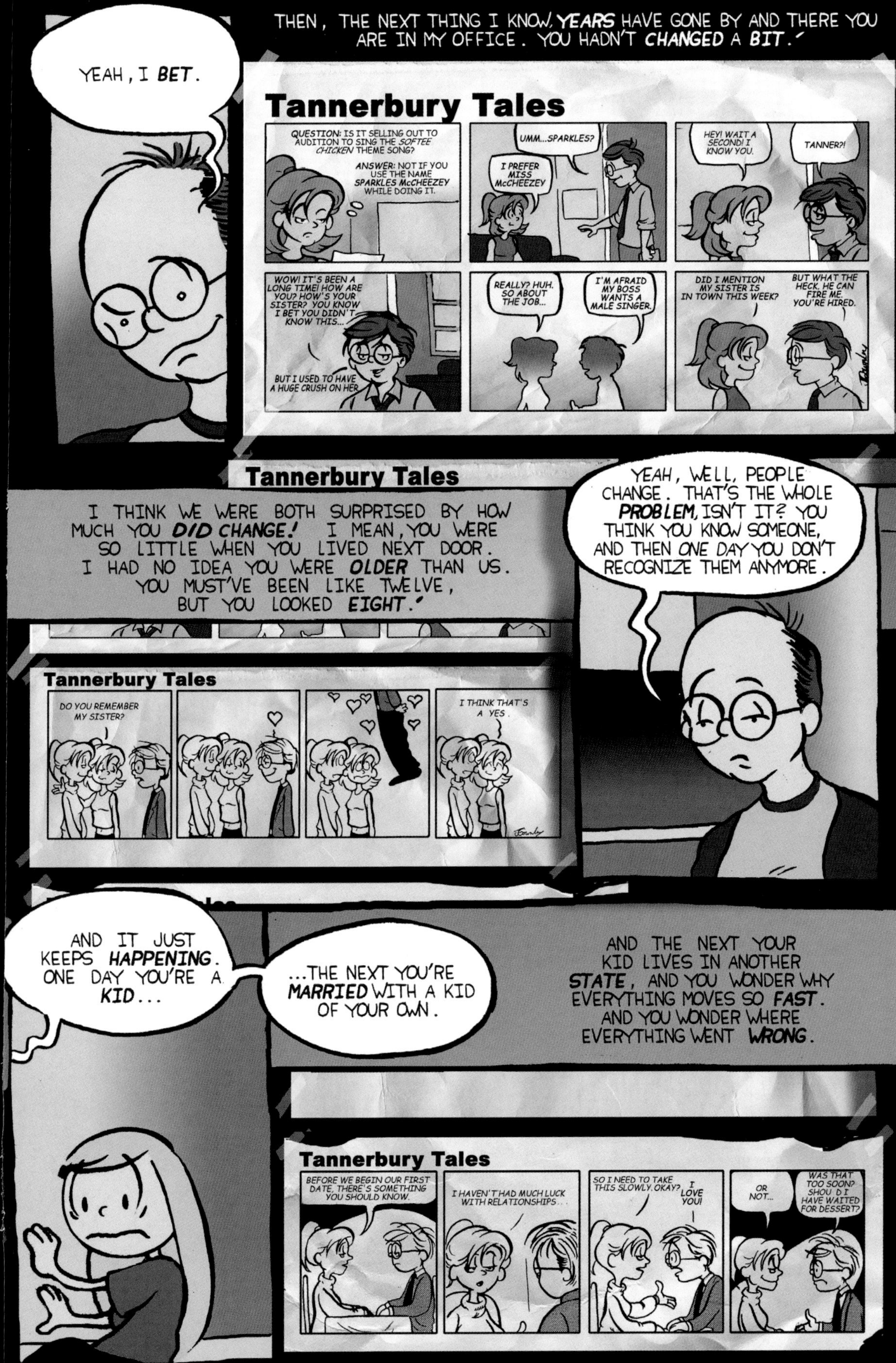
THEN, THE NEXT THING I KNOW, YEARS HAVE GONE BY AND THERE YOU ARE IN MY OFFICE. YOU HADN'T CHANGED A BIT.'
YEAH, I BET.
Tannerbury Tales
QUESTION: IS IT SELLING OUT TO AUDITION TO SING THE SOFTEE CHICKEN THEME SONG?
ANSWER: NOT IF YOU USE THE NAME SPARKLES McCHEEZEY WHILE DOING IT.
UMM...SPARKLES?
I PREFER MISS McCHEEZEY
HEY! WAIT A SECOND! I KNOW YOU.
TANNER?!
WOW! IT'S BEEN A LONG TIME! HOW ARE YOU? HOW'S YOUR SISTER? YOU KNOW I BET YOU DIDN'T KNOW THIS...
BUT I USED TO HAVE A HUGE CRUSH ON HER
REALLY? HUH. SO ABOUT THE JOB...
I'M AFRAID MY BOSS WANTS A MALE SINGER.
DID I MENTION MY SISTER IS IN TOWN THIS WEEK?
BUT WHAT THE HECK. HE CAN FIRE ME. YOU'RE HIRED.
Tannerbury Tales
I THINK WE WERE BOTH SURPRISED BY HOW MUCH YOU DID CHANGE! I MEAN, YOU WERE SO LITTLE WHEN YOU LIVED NEXT DOOR. I HAD NO IDEA YOU WERE OLDER THAN US. YOU MUST'VE BEEN LIKE TWELVE, BUT YOU LOOKED EIGHT.'
YEAH, WELL, PEOPLE CHANGE. THAT'S THE WHOLE PROBLEM, ISN'T IT? YOU THINK YOU KNOW SOMEONE, AND THEN ONE DAY YOU DON'T RECOGNIZE THEM ANYMORE.
Tannerbury Tales
DO YOU REMEMBER MY SISTER?
I THINK THAT'S A YES.
AND IT JUST KEEPS HAPPENING. ONE DAY YOU'RE A KID...
...THE NEXT YOU'RE MARRIED WITH A KID OF YOUR OWN.
AND THE NEXT YOUR KID LIVES IN ANOTHER STATE, AND YOU WONDER WHY EVERYTHING MOVES SO FAST. AND YOU WONDER WHERE EVERYTHING WENT WRONG.
Tannerbury Tales
BEFORE WE BEGIN OUR FIRST DATE, THERE'S SOMETHING YOU SHOULD KNOW.
I HAVEN'T HAD MUCH LUCK WITH RELATIONSHIPS...
SO I NEED TO TAKE THIS SLOWLY. OKAY?
I LOVE YOU!
OR NOT...
WAS THAT TOO SOON? SHOU D I HAVE WAITED FOR DESSERT?

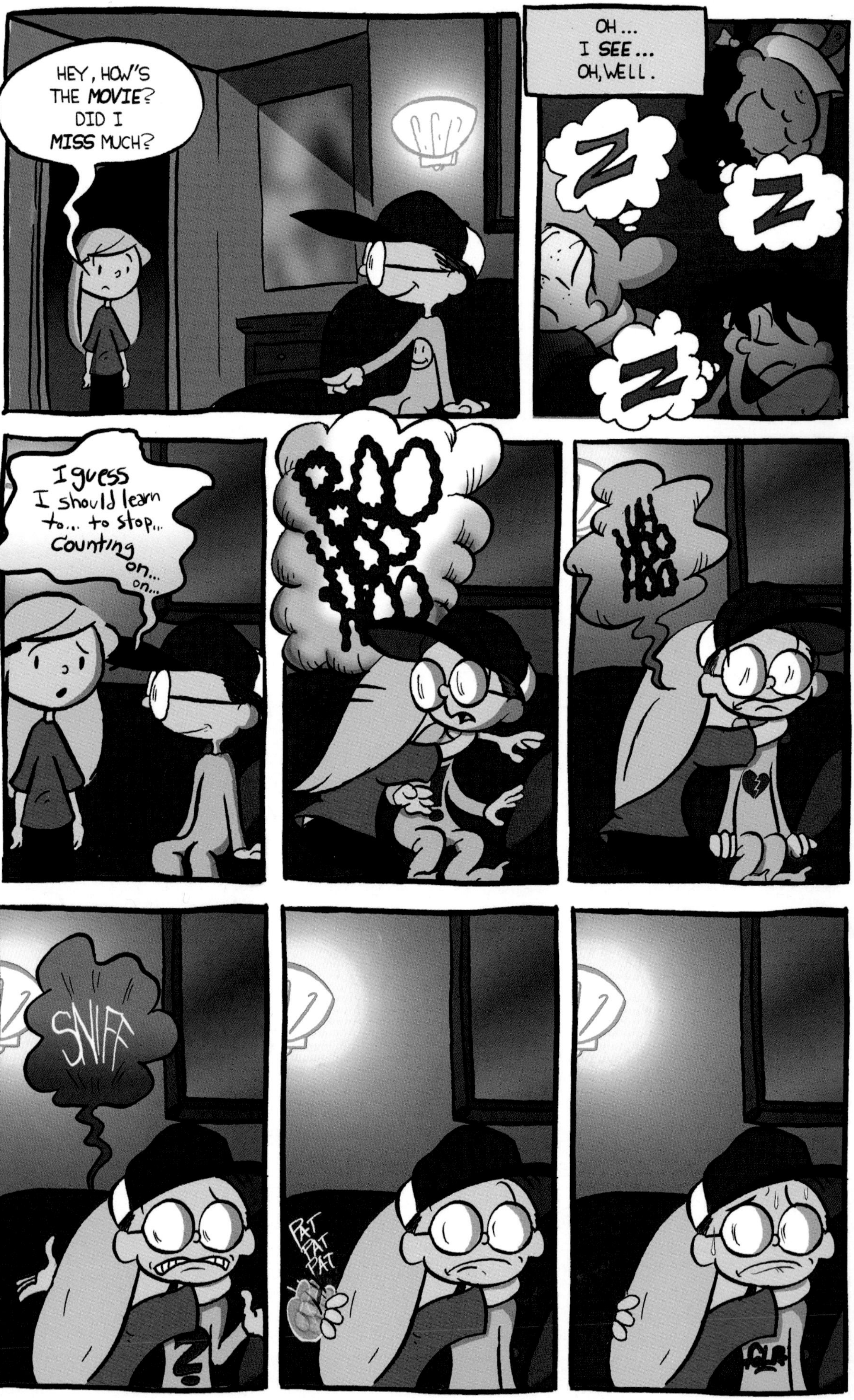
HEY, HOW'S THE MOVIE? DID I MISS MUCH?
OH... I SEE... OH, WELL.
Z
Z
Z
I guess I should learn to... to stop... counting on... on...
BOO HOO HOO
SNIFF
PAT PAT PAT

THE NEXT DAY WAS **GREAT**. DAD TOOK US TO THE **PARK** AND THE **MUSEUM**. AND WE RAN AROUND THE OLD NEIGHBORHOOD PLAYING. BUT OF COURSE...

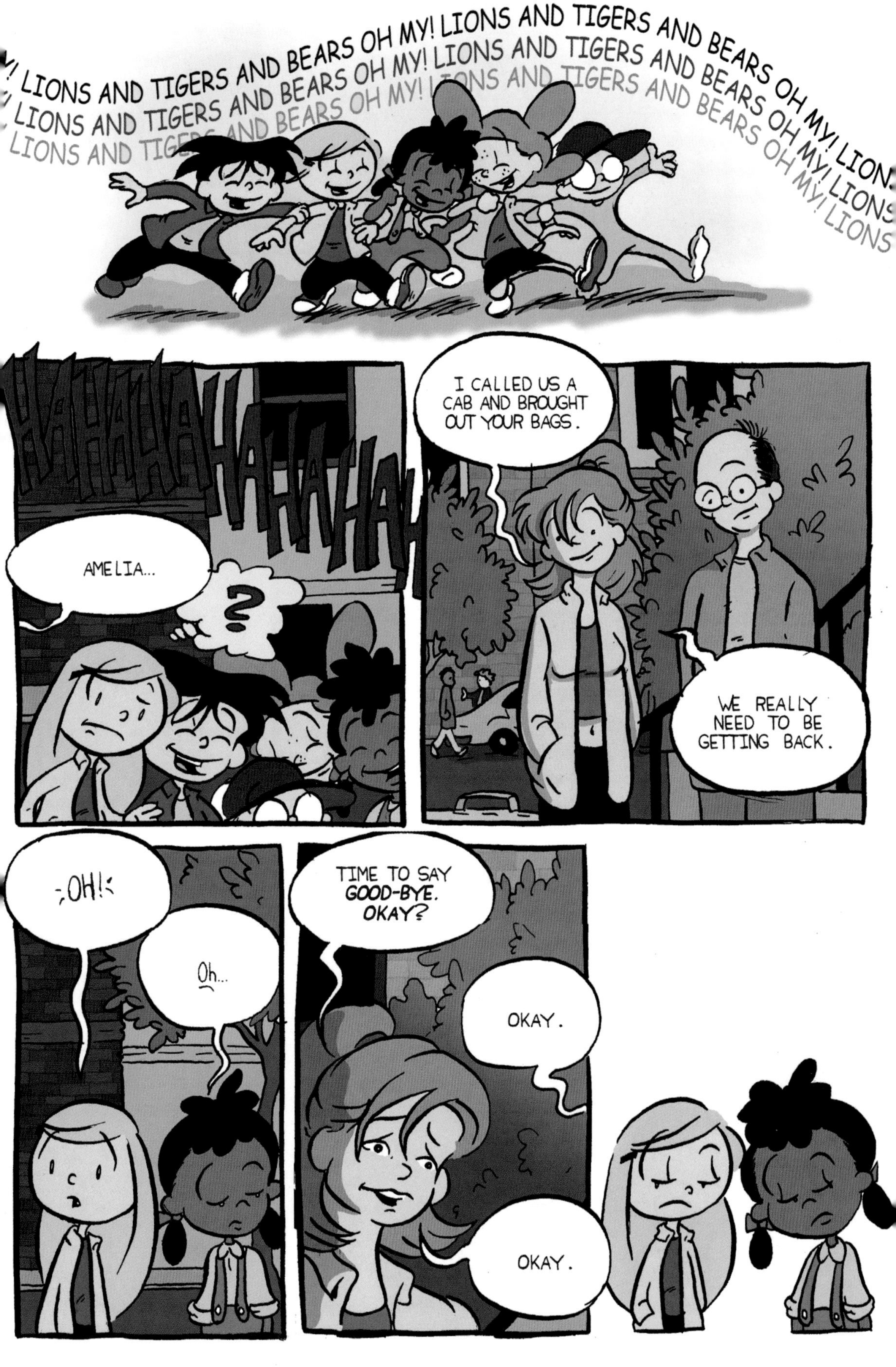
LIONS AND TIGERS AND BEARS OH MY! LIONS AND TIGERS AND BEARS OH MY! LIONS
HAHAHAHAHAHAHAHAH
AMELIA...
?
I CALLED US A CAB AND BROUGHT OUT YOUR BAGS.
WE REALLY NEED TO BE GETTING BACK.
OH!
Oh...
TIME TO SAY GOOD-BYE. OKAY?
OKAY.
OKAY.

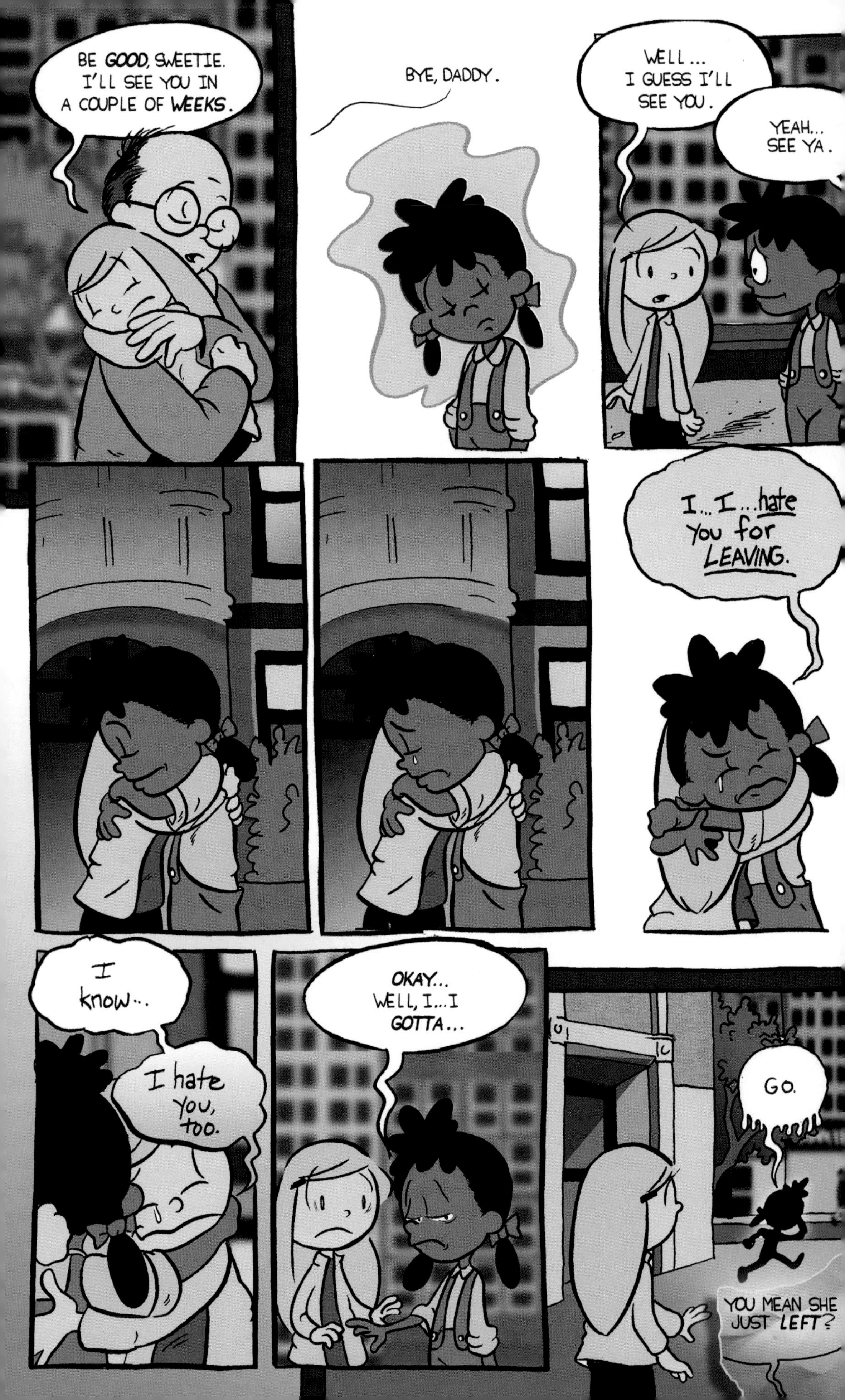
BE GOOD, SWEETIE. I'LL SEE YOU IN A COUPLE OF WEEKS.
BYE, DADDY.
WELL... I GUESS I'LL SEE YOU.
YEAH... SEE YA.
I... I... hate you for LEAVING.
I know...
I hate you, too.
OKAY... WELL, I...I GOTTA...
GO.
YOU MEAN SHE JUST LEFT?

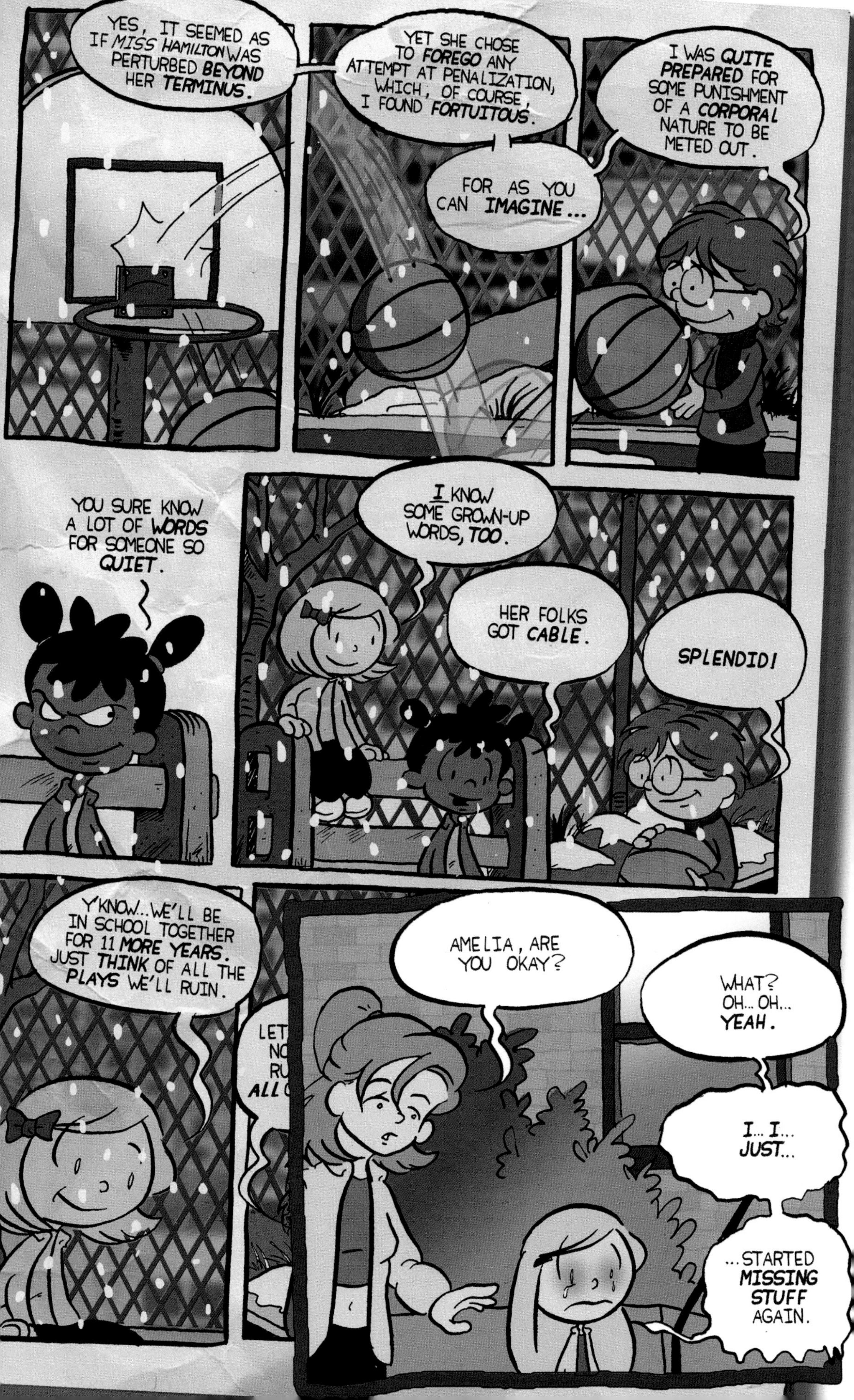
YES, IT SEEMED AS IF MISS HAMILTON WAS PERTURBED BEYOND HER TERMINUS.
YET SHE CHOSE TO FOREGO ANY ATTEMPT AT PENALIZATION, WHICH, OF COURSE, I FOUND FORTUITOUS.
FOR AS YOU CAN IMAGINE...
I WAS QUITE PREPARED FOR SOME PUNISHMENT OF A CORPORAL NATURE TO BE METED OUT.
YOU SURE KNOW A LOT OF WORDS FOR SOMEONE SO QUIET.
I KNOW SOME GROWN-UP WORDS, TOO.
HER FOLKS GOT CABLE.
SPLENDID!
Y'KNOW... WE'LL BE IN SCHOOL TOGETHER FOR 11 MORE YEARS. JUST THINK OF ALL THE PLAYS WE'LL RUIN.
AMELIA, ARE YOU OKAY?
WHAT? OH... OH... YEAH.
I... I... JUST...
...STARTED MISSING STUFF AGAIN.

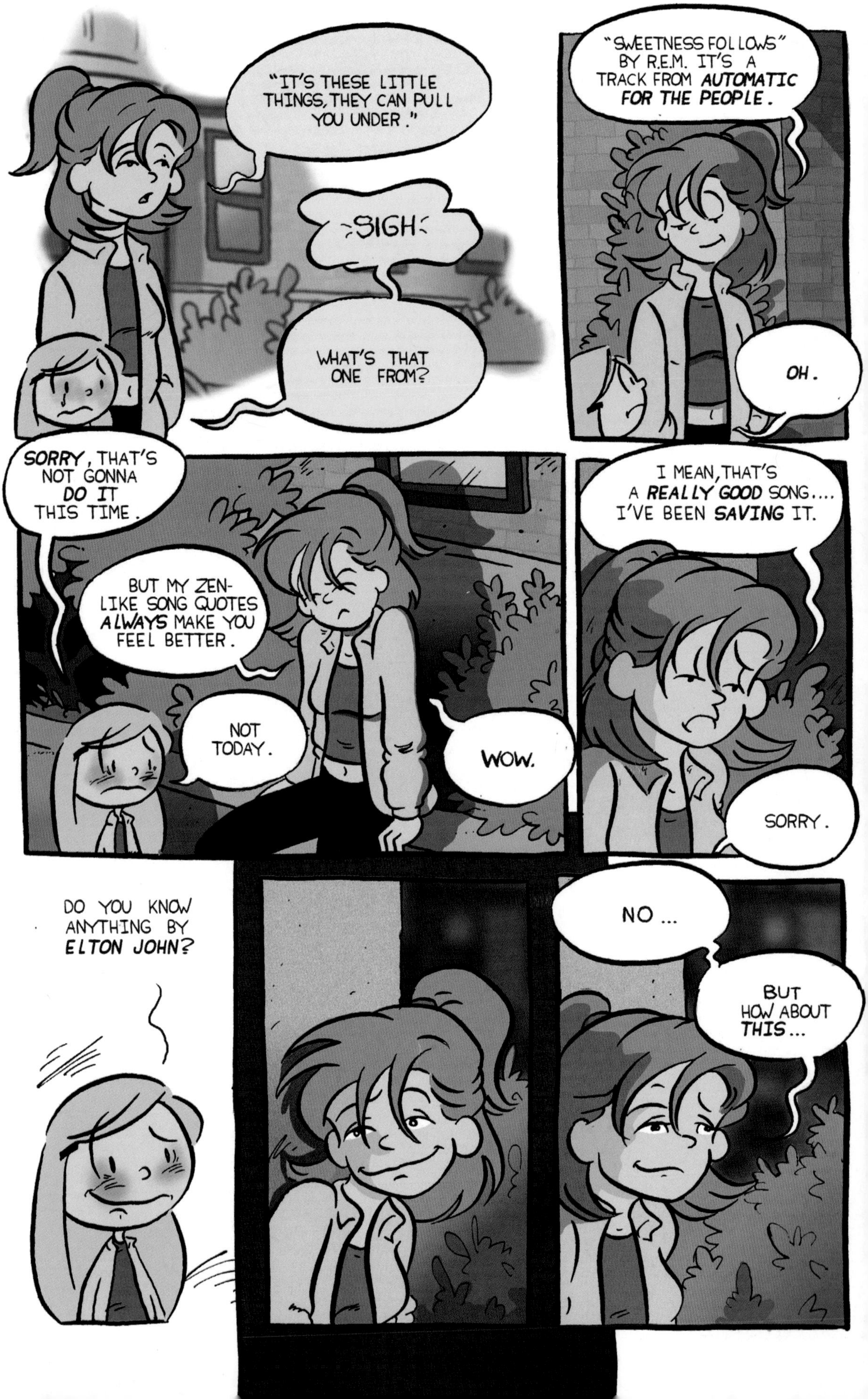
"IT'S THESE LITTLE THINGS, THEY CAN PULL YOU UNDER."
SIGH
WHAT'S THAT ONE FROM?
"SWEETNESS FOLLOWS" BY R.E.M. IT'S A TRACK FROM AUTOMATIC FOR THE PEOPLE.
OH.
SORRY, THAT'S NOT GONNA DO IT THIS TIME.
BUT MY ZEN-LIKE SONG QUOTES ALWAYS MAKE YOU FEEL BETTER.
NOT TODAY.
WOW.
I MEAN, THAT'S A REALLY GOOD SONG.... I'VE BEEN SAVING IT.
SORRY.
DO YOU KNOW ANYTHING BY ELTON JOHN?
NO ...
BUT HOW ABOUT THIS ...

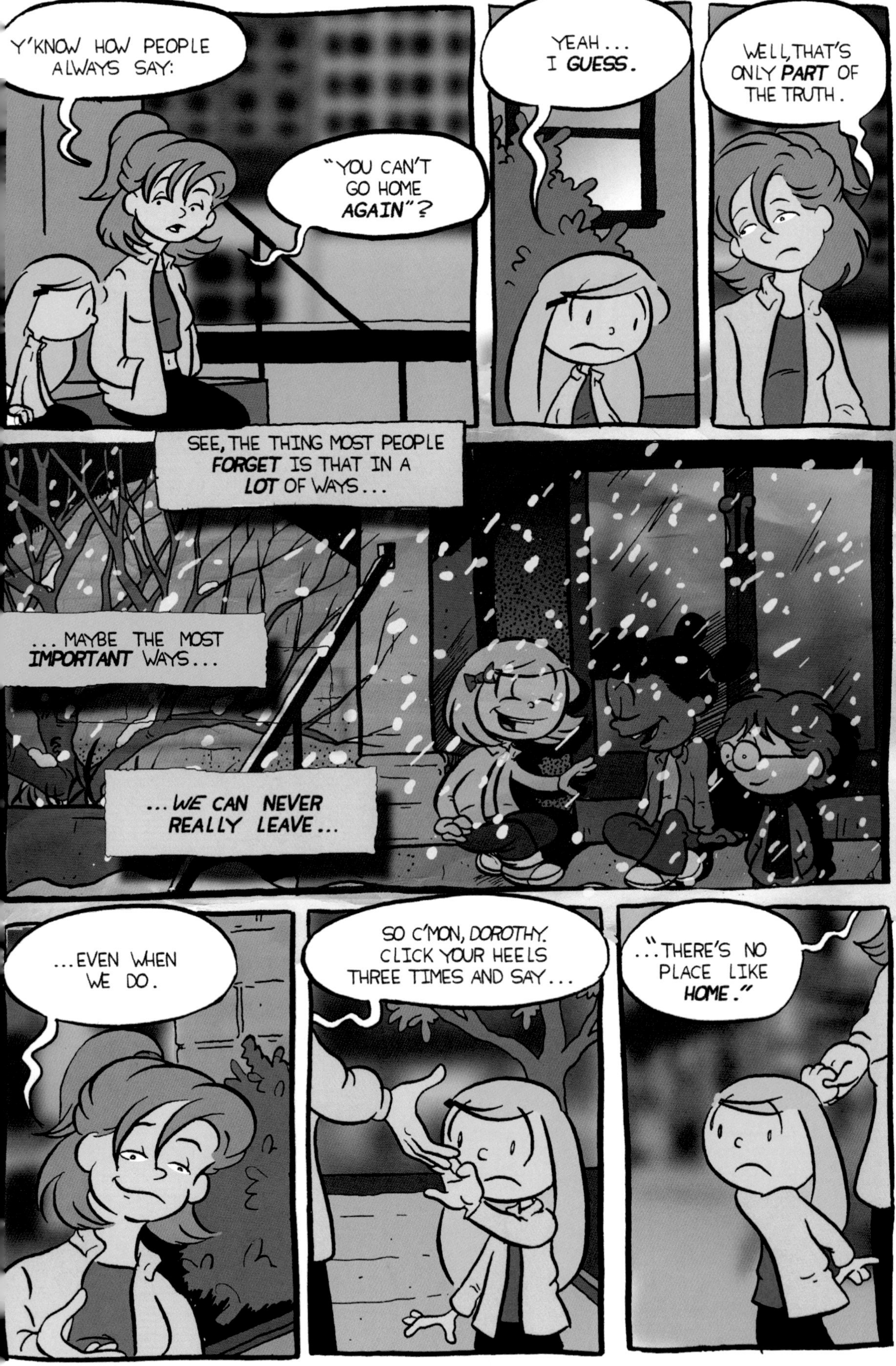

Y'KNOW HOW PEOPLE ALWAYS SAY:
"YOU CAN'T GO HOME AGAIN"?
YEAH... I GUESS.
WELL, THAT'S ONLY PART OF THE TRUTH.
SEE, THE THING MOST PEOPLE FORGET IS THAT IN A LOT OF WAYS...
...MAYBE THE MOST IMPORTANT WAYS...
...WE CAN NEVER REALLY LEAVE...
...EVEN WHEN WE DO.
SO C'MON, DOROTHY. CLICK YOUR HEELS THREE TIMES AND SAY...
..."THERE'S NO PLACE LIKE HOME."

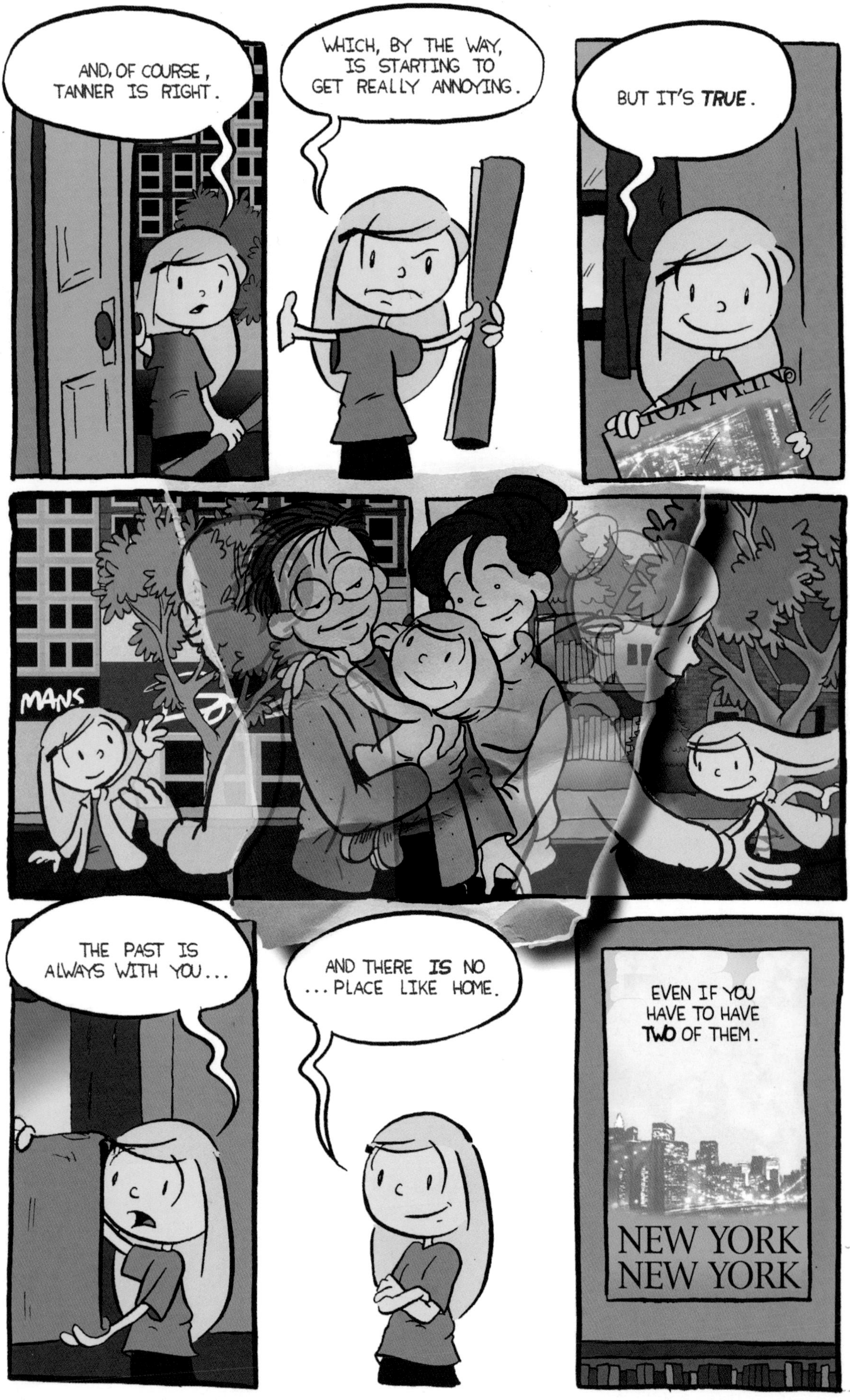
AND, OF COURSE, TANNER IS RIGHT.
WHICH, BY THE WAY, IS STARTING TO GET REALLY ANNOYING.
BUT IT'S **TRUE**.
MANS
THE PAST IS ALWAYS WITH YOU...
AND THERE **IS** NO ...PLACE LIKE HOME.
EVEN IF YOU HAVE TO HAVE **TWO** OF THEM.
NEW YORK NEW YORK